THEY CAME TO F...

Chance Dayton—An ex-cavalry officer and a man of his word. When he says he'll get the job done, he gets it done—with his wits, his fists, or his .44 Colt.

Polly Temple—Bound for Fargo to meet her father, the blond, brown-eyed beauty is headed for a tragedy that will change her life.

Dakota Smith—A shootist without conscience, deadly as a rattlesnake, he has murdered men for the pleasure of it and sees Fargo as his personal killing ground.

Marshal Logan Banner—A lawman driven by revenge, he rides to Fargo seeking Dakota Smith. He won't stop until he has spent his last bullet—the one with the badman's name on it.

Black Claw—On a fanatical quest to win back the lands of his people, he will sacrifice the lives of his own braves to spill more White Eyes' blood.

The Stagecoach Series
Ask your bookseller for the books you have missed

STAGECOACH STATION 21:

FARGO

Hank Mitchum

BCI Created by the producers of
Wagons West, White Indian,
and Saga of the Southwest.

Chairman of the Board: Lyle Kenyon Engel

BANTAM BOOKS
TORONTO · NEW YORK · LONDON · SYDNEY · AUCKLAND

STAGECOACH STATION 21: FARGO

*A Bantam Book / published by arrangement with
Book Creations, Inc.*

Bantam edition / December 1985

*Produced by Book Creations, Inc.
Chairman of the Board: Lyle Kenyon Engel*

ISBN 0-553-25290-9

Published simultaneously in the United States and Canada

---

*Bantam Books are published by Bantam Books, Inc. Its trademark,
consisting of the words "Bantam Books" and the portrayal of a
rooster, is Registered in U.S. Patent and Trademark Office and in
other countries. Marca Registrada. Bantam Books, Inc., 666 Fifth
Avenue, New York, New York 10103.*

PRINTED IN THE UNITED STATES OF AMERICA

H   0 9 8 7 6 5 4 3 2 1

STAGECOACH STATION 21:

FARGO

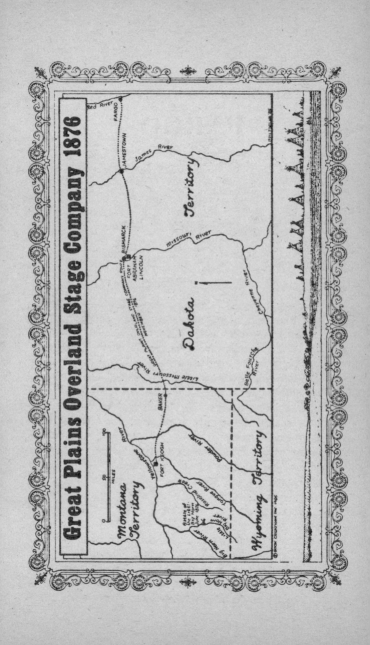

Great Plains Overland Stage Company 1876

Chapter One

Ominous gray clouds rolled across the northern Dakota horizon in the early light of dawn. Chance Dayton, the agent in charge of establishing new routes for the Great Plains Overland Stage Company, turned from the window in the way station. The clouds worried him. He was due in Fort Keogh, in Montana Territory, by the end of next week to board the first stagecoach to travel the new route he had spent the last few months setting up between Fort Keogh and Fargo, Dakota Territory.

"Pete, I hope those clouds don't mean a storm," he said to the stationmaster, Pete Clemmons, a medium-sized man in his early sixties. Dayton, a former cavalry officer, had met Clemmons during the Civil War, when the stationmaster had been the company cook. Later, they had worked together in Kansas for Wells Fargo.

Clemmons placed a steaming plate of steak, eggs, and fried potatoes on the table and then rubbed his right knee. "This old joint says there's a storm a-comin'. However, if I read it right, it's a day or two off."

"I hope it's longer than that," said Dayton, easing his muscular frame onto a chair at the table. "Today is November fifteenth. If no storm gets in my way, I can

1

average fifty miles a day and arrive in Fort Keogh with nearly a week to rest before ol' F.E. Jenkins cracks his whip for that inaugural journey on the twenty-fifth."

Clemmons filled his own plate and joined the thirty-four-year-old Great Plains Overland agent at the table. While both men wolfed down breakfast, the older man studied Dayton with admiration. His two hundred pounds fit nicely on a six-foot-two-inch frame. The man was handsome in a rugged way. He had the kind of face that attracts women . . . symmetrical, with a determined look in his dark-brown eyes and a square-lined jaw to accent the look. He had a head of thick, straight brown hair, with medium-length sideburns and a neatly trimmed mustache. Dayton carried himself with a military posture, and the Colt .44 holstered on his side looked natural there.

The ex-cavalry officer smacked his lips and said, "Pete, you're a great cook. You've been a widower too long. You'd make some woman a wonderful wife!"

Pete laughed. "Speakin' of marriage, Chance, how about yourself? You've never let some little filly put a ring in your nose. How come?"

Dayton's fork, loaded with scrambled eggs, hovered before his mouth while he spoke. "Never have found the right one," he said.

"Well, you'd best be puttin' a hurry on, mister. One of these days you'll get too dadblamed old!"

Dayton swallowed, chuckling, and said, "Man gets in a hurry, he might marry the wrong woman. That'd be worse than not marrying at all."

The clouds to the north seemed stationary half an hour later as Dayton bid the gray-haired man farewell and mounted his horse. The sun had lifted its fiery rim over the eastern horizon, staining Dakota Territory with an orange-red hue. With the rising sun behind him, Dayton headed due west, sitting tall in the saddle, his back ramrod straight.

2

Later that afternoon, Dayton's eyes roamed over the broad, sweeping prairie before him. This morning's conversation with Pete Clemmons had left him a bit melancholy. The old man was right; he ought to find a woman and settle down. Maybe he *had* been too cautious after his heart had been broken back in Ohio, many years ago . . . but he never wanted to feel such anguish again. No one could blame him for that.

He shook his head, as if to dislodge the unpleasant thoughts. No, he knew the way it would be—if and when the right woman appeared, he would know her.

During the long hours of the day, the Great Plains agent stopped periodically to refresh himself and his horse at the relay stations along the route. He knew them well; for the past three months he had been supervising the erection of the stations along the proposed route, in addition to hiring stationmasters and purchasing horses. The company had projected that the stagecoach link between Fort Keogh and Fargo would become quite profitable because it joined the northern part of the West to Minneapolis and the cities of the East.

Also working in favor of the stage route's success were the Indian problems the railroad had been having. The Northern Pacific Railroad had laid track from Minneapolis westward through Fargo, with a railhead at Bismarck. Unhappy with the railroad's intrusion, the Sioux Indians had continuously destroyed large sections of track between Fargo and Bismarck, and had toppled several bridges. The U.S. Army had tried to patrol the stretch, but their ranks were spread too thin.

Sitting Bull and Crazy Horse were still gloating over their victory at Little Big Horn five months earlier in June 1876 and, by tearing up railroad track, were further defying the white men. Northern Pacific officials had finally announced that until the Sioux found something else to occupy themselves, the railhead would be moved back to Fargo. Thus, the Great Plains Overland Stage Company would run their new stagecoach line the entire four hundred and sixty miles from Fort Keogh eastward through Bismarck and on to the railhead at Fargo.

The stage company's president, William Thomas, figured that by late spring or early summer of next year, his company would have six coaches running the route simultaneously. To handle such a volume of traffic, Chance Dayton had placed twenty-three relay stations between Fort Keogh and Fargo at an average of nineteen miles apart. Two were equipped with sleeping quarters for passengers and crew, while the others were designed for a quick change of horses and little more.

The sun began to sink toward the western horizon, and Dayton realized it would be after dark before he reached the next way station. At least when he did, he would have put some fifty-seven miles behind him that day.

Suddenly, off to his right, he saw a cluster of horsemen. At first he thought they were Indians, but a quick look through his binoculars revealed a United States flag flapping in the breeze. It was a cavalry unit of fifteen men, followed by three packhorses.

The unit angled toward Dayton at a canter, raising a light cloud of dust. As they drew abreast, he saw that in the lead was a colonel, flanked by a lieutenant. Directly behind them rode a sergeant, followed by a corporal who supported the red, white, and blue flag. Next to the flagbearer was another corporal, who carried a smaller flag, which identified this squad as a part of B Troop of the Fourth Cavalry. The other ten troopers rode behind, two by two. Dayton knew the Fourth Cavalry was stationed at Fort Buford, some hundred and ten miles northwest of this spot.

The lieutenant raised a hand with military flair and shouted, "Compan-e-e-e-e, halt!" The fifteen-man unit stopped with precision, and Dayton reined in.

4

"Good evening, sir," said the lieutenant. He was a lean man in his late twenties, with a florid face that a thousand suns could not tan. He had a sharp, military manner. "May I introduce you to Colonel Albert Swain, who up until three days ago was commandant at Fort Buford. We are escorting him to Fort Abraham Lincoln, where he will become the new commandant upon arrival."

"Good evening, Colonel." Dayton smiled, almost saluting from habit. "My name is Chance Dayton. I am an agent of the Great Plains Overland Stage Company."

Colonel Albert Swain was a strikingly handsome man in his late fifties, with silver-blue hair and a mustache to match. Nodding, he smiled and said, "Mr. Dayton, this is Lieutenant Marvin Randall." The lieutenant nodded without smiling. Swain added, "And just behind me is Sergeant Bob Grimm."

Grimm, a big man with a ready smile, nodded and said, "Glad to meet you, Mr. Dayton."

"I passed through Bismarck day before yesterday," said the Great Plains agent. "Been there several times but never have visited the fort. It's about eight or nine miles south of the town, I understand."

"That's correct." Swain nodded. Allowing his line of sight to drift past Dayton, he searched the horizon; then meeting Dayton's gaze again, said, "You really should not be out here alone. The Sioux are on the prowl again. Crazy Horse has been shedding some blood."

"Oh?" Dayton blinked. "I thought he got it out of his system when he splattered Custer and the Seventh Cavalry all over the Big Horn Valley."

"I don't know if the Sioux will ever give up spilling white men's blood," Swain commented levelly.

"The railroad has had problems with them since August, tearing up track and burning bridges between Bismarck and Fargo," said Dayton. "On occasion Crazy

Horse has been seen leading them, but I hadn't known of any whites being killed."

"The Oglalas have slaughtered ranchers and farmers recently within a sixty-mile radius of here," said the colonel. "Some of the Fourth Cavalry have had skirmishes with them, but none have sighted the crazy Indian himself." Swain turned his eyes toward the west. The sun was gone. Looking back at the broad-shouldered man, he said, "Are you going much farther this evening, Mr. Dayton?"

Dayton quickly explained his purpose and went on to say that the next relay station, where he planned to spend the night, was some ten or eleven miles to the west.

Fixing Dayton with his commanding eyes, the colonel said, "Mr. Dayton, you are welcome to spend the night with us. We've got some good old army pork and beans, some hardtack, and some coffee. Be happy to share it with you."

Dayton felt the stiffness in his back and legs. He grinned and said, "Think I'll just take you up on it, sir."

The colonel turned to Randall and said, "Lieutenant, we will make camp over here in this shallow ravine."

Randall responded instantly and gave command for the squad to move to the draw and dismount.

Dusk seemed to fall quickly over the Dakota plains as the cavalry squad set up camp. The wind sprang up and snapped at the walls of the small tents while the iron stakes that held them were being driven into the frozen earth. The tents were placed in a circle, and a large fire was built inside the ring.

The temperature dropped considerably as darkness closed in. With collars pulled up and backs bent against the wind, the cavalry squad and their guest ate the evening meal. The firelight cast phantom shadows across the faces of the men as they huddled close to its warmth.

During the meal, Dayton told Colonel Swain and

Lieutenant Randall of his part in the Civil War. When he revealed what battles he had been in, the men discovered mutual acquaintances. The conversation turned to Dayton's stagecoach experience, and the colonel showed an interest in the business. Dayton was glad to supply answers to his questions, giving details of his five years with Wells Fargo and his six years with Great Plains.

"You have a family, Dayton?" queried the colonel. "A wife and children, I mean."

"No, sir," Dayton replied. "I'm not married."

Swain grinned. "I'd think a good-looking chap like you would have been trapped by some scheming female long ago."

Dayton shook his head as the wind whipped against the fire, throwing sparks toward the black sky. "I've had an opportunity or two, but just never have found the woman with whom I wanted to share the rest of my life," he answered. Turning the tables, he said, "What about you, Colonel?"

"Me?"

"Do you have a family?"

"Oh, yes. I have one daughter. My wife died of pneumonia in the winter of '72. Had a son. He was killed when he was eleven years old. Horse threw him."

"I'm sorry, sir," Dayton said with genuine feeling. Changing the subject, he asked about Swain's new assignment. Fort Abraham Lincoln was the largest military post in the Dakotas. Its commandant carried great prestige in military circles.

They discussed the Indian situation and Crazy Horse's new uprising. The men talked of the battle at Little Big Horn and how Crazy Horse had lived up to his name, acting like a madman. Some of the mutilation of the Seventh Cavalry's dead had been worse than savage.

Sergeant Bob Grimm puffed on his pipe and nodded

in affirmation. "I talked to Lieutenant Jim Bradley, commander of Gibbon's scouts," he said. "He and his men were the first to ride up on the scene. Bradley told me how he saw white objects dotting the hillside. They turned out to be the naked bodies of two hundred and fifty men, white as marble in the sunlight, except for their tanned faces and hands. They were speckled, spattered, and smeared with blood. Most of them had their throats cut. Some of the bodies were chopped up so bad they could not be identified."

Dayton shook his head in disbelief.

Grimm continued. "Captain Myles Keogh's face was nothing but raw meat. Bradley said they identified him by the crucifix he wore around his neck. Keogh's wounded horse was the only living thing left on the battlefield."

"What about Custer?" Dayton asked. "How bad did Crazy Horse mutilate him?"

Bob Grimm was fighting the wind, attempting to relight his pipe. Giving up, he said, "Funny thing about that, Mr. Dayton. They stripped the general naked but didn't even scalp him. The only wounds on his body were two bullet holes, one in his left temple and one in his chest."

"His *temple?*"

"I know what you're thinking," Grimm said, "but suicide was absolutely ruled out. There were no powder burns around either wound. The general died with Sioux bullets in him. Bradley thinks that Crazy Horse made sure General Custer's body was *not* mutilated. He held Custer in such contempt that he disdained him as insignificant and not worth mutilating. But that didn't hold true for the body of his brother, Tom Custer."

"Oh? I knew that Tom Custer had been commissioned into the regular army," Dayton said, "but I was not aware that he was under his brother's command."

"Both of them wanted it that way," Colonel Swain

spoke up. "Tom Custer showed a whole lot of courage in battle. George wanted him by his side at all times."

Dayton nodded, then asked Grimm, "So what happened to Tom's body?"

The sergeant tightened his hat against the wind and replied, "They scalped him by small sections, until the only hair left was on the nape of his neck. Then they used heavy rocks to crush his skull. After that, they . . . they opened his chest and cut out his heart."

Dayton's face paled.

"Then they shot him full of arrows," added Grimm. "Bradley said Tom's body bristled with so many arrows that he looked like a porcupine."

Dayton shivered. "They don't call him Crazy Horse for nothing, do they?"

"He's crazy all right," Lieutenant Marvin Randall replied, "but not nearly as vicious as Black Claw."

"Black Claw? I haven't run across the name before," Dayton said.

"Black Claw is a renegade—even Crazy Horse can't control him. He was raised in Crazy Horse's tribe, but he surpasses his leader in ruthlessness. From what I heard, he not only killed a good many men at Little Big Horn but he went around mutilating corpses after his comrades had finished with them. He's also notorious for showing no mercy to women and children, not even to those of his own tribe who have displeased him." The lieutenant shook his head.

Dayton poured himself more of the hot, black coffee. "Black Claw . . . that's an ominous-sounding name."

"Got it by killing a huge black bear when he was just a boy," Randall explained. "Did it singlehandedly, with just a boy's knife. To this day he wears a necklace of the black bear's claws around his neck."

No one spoke during the next minutes as the fire's flames cast a red glow over the men's faces. Then Randall spoke again, as if to close the subject: "He's a madman, Black Claw is. . . . He ought to be shot like a rabid dog."

Daylight came with a fierce, biting wind. The smell of snow was in the air, and a heavy arch of solid gray spanned the sky. On the northern horizon, thick masses of black-bellied clouds were moving southward.

The cavalrymen had rolled up their tents and placed them on the backs of the packhorses. Breakfast was devoured quickly. Chance Dayton tightened the cinch of his saddle and then strode over to the silver-haired officer. Removing one glove, he extended his hand, saying, "Colonel Swain, it has been a pleasure meeting you. I'll be on my way, now."

Swain met his grip. "The feeling is mutual, Dayton. Anytime you are passing through Bismarck and have time to visit the fort, I would be honored to have you as my guest."

"Thank you, sir," the Great Plains agent said with a smile. "I'll do just that." On his way toward his horse, the dark-haired Dayton said good-bye to the sergeant and waved to the men. He swung into the saddle and guided his horse out of the ravine.

The figures came up from the frozen ground as if they had been a part of it. The prairie was suddenly alive with Indians, on foot, advancing at a dead run. An arrow hissed by Dayton's left ear as he wheeled his mount and shouted, "Colonel! Colonel! Indians attacking!"

The cavalrymen were standing beside their horses, waiting for the command to mount, when Dayton's voice cut the air and he came riding back.

Colonel Swain was already in the saddle, as was the lieutenant. The Oglala Sioux opened fire as they reached the edge of the ravine. Swain took the first bullet while the troopers were scrambling for their carbines. Dayton saw the slug enter the colonel's forehead: he was dead before he toppled from the saddle.

The sudden burst of gunfire and the war cries of the Sioux sent the cavalry horses into a panic. Nickers and whinnies blended with the thunderous sounds of Indian yells, hissing arrows, and blazing guns.

Dayton dived from his saddle, ripping the Colt .44 from its holster. He watched as the army packhorses topped the crest of the ravine and disappeared, only a canvas knapsack remaining in their dust. Flattening himself on the ground, he fired point-blank at a Sioux who was charging straight for him, rifle poised. The Indian took the bullet square in the chest and dropped like a rock.

Gun smoke filled the cold morning air. Both red and white men were falling on all sides.

Dayton saw an Indian drive a knife into the back of Lieutenant Marvin Randall, who had just shot a Sioux through the heart. As the Indian pulled out the knife, Dayton blew him into eternity.

It was bedlam. The shouting and cursing of blue-uniformed men joined with the war whoops and death screams of those in buckskins. Knives flashed, and blood flowed.

Dayton emptied his revolver, downing two more Indians. Jamming the gun back in its holster, he picked up the carbine of a dead trooper. He jacked a shell into the chamber and fired through the smoke at the outline of an Indian. The brave dropped his knife, clutched the wound, and fell. When the smoke cleared momentarily, Dayton saw big Bob Grimm turn and smile at him. Dayton's shot had saved the sergeant from being stabbed.

While Grimm was still smiling, another Oglala Sioux, seeming to come from nowhere, leaped forward and drove a knife into his side, near his heart. Dayton worked the lever of the carbine, aimed it at the Indian, and pulled the trigger. The dead, dry sound of the hammer snapping on an empty chamber seemed louder than if the gun had fired.

The warrior screamed a cry of conquest as he jerked the knife from Grimm's side, letting the sergeant's body sag to the ground. Then the Indian whirled and lunged at Dayton, bloody knife swinging. Dayton dodged the blade and reversed the carbine in his hands, gripping the end of the barrel and, wielding it like a club, brought it around violently in a full arc. It met the Indian's skull with a savage, crushing sound. The Indian was undoubtedly dead.

Abruptly, from out of the heavy smoke, another Indian threw himself screaming at Dayton, knocking the Great Plains agent flat. Dayton rolled on the ground, his senses reeling. Before he could clear his vision, the brave was on top of him, slashing wildly with a knife.

He felt the blade tear at his left forearm. Then, flat on his back, he watched the Sioux straddle him and raise the knife to drive it into his chest. Without a moment's hesitation, Dayton brought up both knees as hard as he could, striking the Indian's rump. Thrown off balance, the Indian stabbed the knife solidly into the ground above Dayton's head, but he quickly yanked it loose, ready for another try.

Dayton saw the danger and grabbed the wrist of the Indian's knife hand. The two men struggled as the blade trembled in the Indian's hand only two inches from Dayton's chest. The brave's eyes bulged wildly as he grunted with effort through his clenched teeth.

Dayton knew he must do something fast; the Indian was on top and clearly had the advantage. Summoning strength from somewhere within him, the ex-cavalry officer bowed his back, twisted violently, and rolled free. Instantly, he was on his feet. The Indian bounded upward, snarling, his eyes wild, blade out in front. Quickly, he closed in.

The tip of the blade cut cloth as Dayton stepped back, and before the Sioux could manage another swing, Dayton lunged in, seizing the Indian's wrist again. They were deadlocked, nose to nose, both sucking hard for air. Dayton could feel the hot, foul breath of the Indian in his face.

Putting everything he had into his effort, Dayton slowly twisted the wrist of his opponent until the blade was angled toward the Sioux's belly at belt level. The Indian's endurance was waning. Dayton saw the shadow of death in the man's eyes.

Then the blade was in the Sioux's belly, all the way to the haft, and Dayton ripped upward. The brave clenched his teeth, batted his eyes, and emitted a deep grunt. His knees buckled. Dayton felt a warm, sticky fluid moisten his hand as he let the Indian drop, the knife still buried in his midsection.

Taking huge gulps of cold air into his lungs, Dayton ran a bloody, tattered sleeve over his sweaty face. It was then that he realized the battle was over. The smoke had cleared; the noise had stopped. Bloody bodies were scattered everywhere, some lying in grotesque heaps, others sprawled in lifeless contortions on the frozen, windswept ground.

Blinking against the stinging sweat in his eyes, Dayton saw a lone Indian running and stumbling westward out on the prairie. He must be headed for wherever they had stashed their horses.

"Oh, no, you don't!" the ex-soldier said under his breath. "If you get away, you'll bring others!" His eyes searched the ground. A carbine lay nearby. Picking it up, he checked the magazine, saw there were two bullets left, and rammed a shell home into the chamber. He ran hard toward the fleeing Sioux, then stopped. He took careful aim. He wanted to stop the Indian without killing him.

The Indian was apparently unaware of Dayton's pursuit until he heard the sharp crack of the rifle and saw the bullet chew dirt near his feet. He stopped abruptly; Dayton watched as the man turned his head. "Stop right there!" Dayton yelled.

The Indian paused only for a few seconds and then wheeled and ran for all he was worth. Dayton shook his head and shouldered the rifle again. When he fired, the gun bucked against him. The Indian stopped, arched his back, clawed for the sky, and fell flat.

Chapter Two

Dayton dropped the empty rifle and slowly turned toward the shallow ravine where he and the cavalry squad had camped the night before. The ground was littered with fallen men. He realized abruptly that neither his horse nor any other was in sight. Then something else touched his awareness—snow and sleet pellets were striking him in the face.

The ex-cavalry officer peered again at the scattered bodies. Were they all dead? Had no one else survived? His gaze fell on Colonel Albert Swain, the man's sightless eyes looking like opaque agates staring at the sullen, gray sky, his forehead centered with a dark hole. Kneeling, Dayton closed the colonel's eyelids as snow settled in the dead man's silver hair.

The bulky body of Sergeant Bob Grimm lay on top of a dead Sioux. Apparently Grimm had not been dead when he had first fallen from the knife wound in his side, Dayton realized, for he had crawled to a different spot and collapsed in a heap on the Indian's corpse.

Careful examination of the other soldiers revealed that all fifteen were dead. Then he counted eighteen lifeless Sioux, including the one he had shot out on the prairie. Brushing snow from his hair, he looked around for his hat and found it near the body of a trooper with an arrow through his throat.

As Dayton picked up the hat, he realized that his right hand was still sticky with the blood of the Sioux who had almost done him in. Walking a few feet to where another dead Indian lay, he knelt and wiped the blood on the buckskin coat of the corpse.

Standing up, he pulled five bullets from his gunbelt, loaded his revolver, placed the hammer on the empty chamber, and holstered it. At that instant he became aware of the pain in his left arm. It had not occurred to him that the blood on his tattered coat sleeve was his own.

Working his arm out of the sleeve, Dayton examined the two-inch gash across his forearm. It was still bleeding. He wished he had some medical supplies to clean and properly bandage the wound. Then he remembered the knapsack he had seen on the ground at the crest of the ravine—the one that had fallen from one of the packhorses as they ran away. There might just be a medical kit in that canvas bag.

Rubbing snowflakes from his eyelashes, Dayton turned in the direction of the knapsack. As he started to move, he heard a moan. Looking about quickly, he ran his eyes over the motionless corpses, now white with snow. He knew the noise had to have come from one of the Indians; he had examined all the soldiers and found them dead.

The moan met his ears again. Swinging his gaze in the direction of the sound, he saw a young brave, no older than twenty, who was lying prone. Just then the brave stirred and rolled his head. With his gun drawn, Dayton moved to where the Indian lay, and stood over him. There was a large lump, split and bleeding, on the side of the brave's head. Dayton's eyes also caught sight of blood on the Sioux's left buckskin pantleg, where a bullet had punctured the thigh.

The long-haired Indian moaned again, rolling and lifting his head. His eyes batted for a moment and then opened, slowly focusing on the towering figure that stood over him. When the Indian saw the revolver in Dayton's hand, he raised his head slightly, then eased it back to the cold ground. The dismal recognition that he was about to die seemed to register in his dark eyes.

"Do you speak English?" Dayton said.

Struggling again to raise his head, the Indian said, "I . . . I learn at mission school."

Dayton knelt down beside him, tossing aside a rifle that had lain within the dark-skinned man's reach. Noting that the scabbard on the wounded brave's side was empty, and seeing no knife on the ground, the ex-cavalry officer helped him sit up.

While the Indian's clouded eyes watched him warily, Dayton said, "Looks like you and I are the only two left alive."

The young brave put a hand to the lump on his head, touching it gingerly, and then looked at the bloody spot on his leg.

"We're both banged up some," Dayton said. "I think there might be some medical supplies over there in an army knapsack. I was just about to go after it when I heard you. Just sit here a minute, and I'll go get it. Maybe we can stop the bleeding in your leg."

The Indian looked at the tall man in disbelief. "You . . . you will help me?"

"You're hurt, aren't you?"

"Yes . . . but we are enemies. Why do you—?"

"We'll talk about it later," Dayton said, standing up. "You relax. I'll be right back."

The knapsack proved to contain food and a quart of whiskey, but no medical supplies. The wounded Sioux, his eyes displaying caution and bewilderment, watched Dayton cut away the buckskin pantleg and examine the wound. The bullet had passed through the flesh on the outside of the thigh. He had lost a good deal of blood, but since the bullet had not lodged in the leg, the wound would not prove serious if infection did not set in.

Dayton warned the Indian of the pain that was coming, then poured whiskey into the open wound. The man tried desperately not to show that the whiskey burned like fire, but despite his effort, he soon became dizzy and passed out. While he was unconscious, Dayton bandaged the leg with the shirt of a dead soldier and cleaned the head wound, wrapping it tightly. After that, he treated his own wounded left arm. Within minutes the Indian regained consciousness.

The wind was blowing hard now, and the snow was getting heavier. Dayton knew that both of them were doomed if they did not find shelter from the storm. Suddenly, he remembered a gully he had passed the day before. It was a straight-edged crevice in the earth, some ten or twelve feet wide, and with an overhang along one side. Possibly it would provide shelter enough for them to wait out the storm. But his heart sank when he remembered it was at least a mile back. Silently, he cursed the horses for running away.

Kneeling beside the Indian, Dayton said, "We must get out of this storm. I know a place about a mile east of here. It's not much, but it's better than this."

As Dayton raised the brave to a sitting position, the Indian said, "I cannot make it. You go on. Take shelter."

"I can't leave you here to freeze to death," said Dayton. "I'll carry you. We can make it."

"Wait," the Indian said. "I do not understand. I am your enemy. Why—?"

"No time to answer questions," Dayton cut in. "We've got to get moving."

Blinking against the driving snow, he hoisted the wounded Indian over his shoulder and rose. After struggling against the increasing wind for nearly an hour, he finally reached the gully and placed the wounded man in it. It was dry under the overhang, which was closed in on three sides and low enough in the gully to be out of the harsh wind.

Making the Sioux warrior as comfortable as possible, Dayton said, "It's going to get very cold, I'll wager. You must be wrapped in something warm. I'll go back and get some coats."

The Indian started to protest, but Dayton silenced him with his dark brown eyes and disappeared into the howling storm.

Upon his return from the site of the massacre, Dayton found the Indian in a fevered chill. He gave him a healthy swig of whiskey and then took some himself. He had taken five coats from the dead cavalrymen, expecting the garments to be enough to keep himself and the Indian warm, but upon returning and finding his patient so chilled, he wrapped the quivering man in all five, adding his own. Hunkering under the ledge, Dayton periodically worked his arms and legs to keep warm and to keep the circulation going.

As the hours passed, the snowfall subsided, but the wind continued to howl and whine around the edges of the shelter. The Indian's teeth stopped chattering, and he told Dayton that the pain in his leg had eased. His eyes became clear. He looked at Dayton from the bundle of coats and said, "You will die of the cold, white eyes. Put your own coat on. I am warm now."

The Sioux studied Dayton quizzically as the stage company agent laid a palm on his brow, saying, "You do seem to be better. If you're sure you're warm enough, I will take my coat."

The Indian assured him that five coats were sufficient, and Dayton slipped his own on, telling the Indian that he was going to gather some wood. Darkness was coming soon, and they would need a fire.

Later, as night closed in around them, Dayton hunkered by the fire. He had built it under the edge of the overhang, so the smoke would lift skyward. The two men ate food from the knapsack, which contained beef jerky, beans, dried pork, hardtack, and coffee, along with tin plates, cups, pots, and utensils. Melted snow provided water for cooking the beans and brewing the coffee.

The Indian remained somber as he chomped the food. When Dayton smiled at him, the injured man remained aloof and stoical, but slowly his defenses crumbled.

"You will feel much better when you get your stomach full," Dayton said amiably.

The Indian eyed the dark-haired man with uncertainty and said in his deep voice, "Why you do this, white eyes? I am your enemy. I ride with Black Claw. As Oglala Sioux, I am sworn to kill you."

"I know that," replied Dayton.

The Indian's dark eyes squinted with wonder. "You could have killed me there on the plain. Or walked away and let me die. Yet not only did you spare my life, you saved it. You risked your own life to give me your coat. Why? Do you not know I must kill you when my strength returns?"

"I am gambling that you won't try that," said the broad-shouldered man.

"I *must*," came the throaty reply.

"Because you are Sioux, because you are my enemy, or because you ride for Black Claw?"

The Indian fixed him with a hard stare. Dayton had boxed him into a corner. Not all Sioux were killing white men without provocation. His band of Oglala Sioux were vicious because of their leader, Black Claw, who had infected them with a relentless hatred for whites.

The brave clamped his jaw, grinding his teeth. Dayton's gaze held him hard, as he waited for an answer. Then it came.

"Because I ride for Black Claw," he said evenly.

"Does Black Claw do your thinking for you, or can you think for yourself?"

The Indian pondered it for a moment. "North Wind can think for himself," he answered flatly.

"Your name is North Wind?"

"Yes."

"Listen, North Wind," Dayton said. "I don't blame the Indians for their resentment of the white man. You have a perfect right to feel anger toward us. This is your land; your people have been here for ages. We whites have come where we were not invited."

North Wind could not believe his ears. Here was a hated white admitting that his kind had done the Indian wrong. The stoniness of his features began to soften.

Dayton continued. "White men have killed off your buffalo. They have tried to starve you out. They have broken treaties and lied to you. They have attempted to run you off your land. This is wrong."

In his deep voice, North Wind said, "Are you not one of them, white eyes? Are you not a soldier?"

"No, I'm not," replied Dayton. "I am not military, nor am I a government man. I live and serve under the United States flag, but I do not condone what some of my people have done to the Indians. I say some, be-cause we are not all responsible for what has been done. Many like myself want to live in peace with your people. We do not want to kill you, nor push you off your land."

The dark eyes flashed. "You killed Oglalas today!"

"Only in self-defense," retorted the tall man. "I killed to keep from being killed. I am ashamed of what has been done to your people. The only thing I can do as an individual is show that my heart is right in the matter."

The words took effect in North Wind's mind, and the fire died in his eyes. Nodding slowly, he said, "North Wind believes you."

Dayton smiled. Leaning close, he said, "North Wind, I want you to understand that I consider you my brother. Though our backgrounds are different, and our skin is

21

different, we are both human beings, created by the same Great Spirit. You are my brother."

This was a new and different experience for North Wind, who had been taught that all white men were bad, and that, without exception, they hated the Indian. He had found it difficult at times to accept the bloody philosophy of killing every white man, woman, and child just because they were white. But never had he voiced his thoughts, for to do so would have meant that he was disloyal to his own kind—a traitor. Here was a white man who shared these feelings.

A warm sensation ignited in the center of North Wind's breast and spread through his upper body. A smile tugged at the corners of his mouth, and he looked at Chance Dayton and spoke one word: "*Brother.*"

The white man smiled and repeated the word.

The remaining food replaced in the knapsack, Dayton threw some wood onto the red-hot coals and moved to North Wind's side. "Let's take a look at the wound," he said.

While the white man unwrapped the damaged leg, the Indian shifted his position. Suddenly his arm bumped the hard object that was strapped to his chest under the buckskin shirt. *The spare knife!* Under Black Claw's tutoring, North Wind wore concealed on his body a small knife with a five-inch blade when going into battle. Until this moment, he had forgotten about it.

His right hand moved under the coats to the thin bulge under his shirt, and his fingers traced the outline of the knife. He could easily slip it out and plunge the blade into the white man's body.

Abruptly, his conscience smote him for even allowing such a thought, and he silently scolded himself. This man had saved his life and called him brother. North Wind must not even think of killing him.

Dayton poured more whiskey on the Indian's wound.

Enduring the pain, North Wind watched him rewind the makeshift bandage. "White eyes must have a name. What is the name?"

"My name is Chance Dayton."

"What means *Chance Dayton?*"

"It doesn't mean anything," replied the white man. "Our names do not always have a meaning like those of the Indian."

"I give it meaning," said North Wind. "Chance Dayton means *white-man-whose-heart-is-right.*"

Dayton smiled, lines creasing at the corners of his eyes. "I'll accept that," he said. He eyed the other man for a moment, and then asked, "Were you with Black Claw when Crazy Horse attacked Custer?"

North Wind nodded. "Yes, I was there."

"Some battle, huh?"

"It did not last long. Crazy Horse took Yellow Hair by surprise. Yellow Hair was one of the first to die. No longer does he talk with lying tongue and say Sioux are weak and poor fighters. Yellow Hair found out."

A triumphant light glistened in the Indian's dark eyes. Dayton wanted to ask why General Custer's body had not been mutilated or scalped, but he let it pass. Instead, he satisfied another curiosity. "Let me ask you something about Black Claw."

North Wind met his eyes, ready to defend his chief.

"Is it true that he got the name from killing a bear?"

North Wind's eyes flashed. "Any man can kill a bear," he said. "But Black Claw, he killed Bear-Who-Fools, about whom many grandfathers of our tribe speak with reverence. Bear-Who-Fools was known for generations for his skill at eluding the most accomplished hunters of the Oglala Sioux. But Black Claw, when he had seen only nine winters, released the spirit of Bear-Who-Fools, using only the small knife of a boy. For that deed he took the name Black Claw. Around his neck the claws of Bear-Who-Fools still hang."

Pride was evident in North Wind's dark, deep-set

eyes as he added, "Black Claw is greatest warrior! Blue-coats find out!"

Chance Dayton said no more about the infamous leader. Instead, he brought up the subject of the missing horses, saying that in the morning he would go out and see if he could locate them. He also said he would take North Wind to a doctor and have his leg treated properly. The Indian, though, insisted on riding back to his own camp before daybreak and asked Dayton to find him a horse right away.

Dayton just smiled in reply as the icy wind howled around the sides of the dirt fortress. After adding wood to the fire, he removed the bandage and poured whiskey into the Indian's wound one more time, then covered him for the night. "You just get some sleep," he said kindly. "You'll be better off here for the night. I'm going out for some more wood."

North Wind managed a tight smile. "You must sleep, also," he countered. "North Wind will remain awake part of the night and feed the fire so that Chance Dayton may sleep."

Dayton slipped out into the night without comment. Upon his return, he saw that North Wind was, indeed, asleep. Building up the fire, he lay back and thought of the day's brutal events . . . of the fifteen cavalrymen whose bodies lay out there in the shallow ravine, frozen and covered with snow. And, of course, seventeen of Black Claw's men lay out there, too. *What a useless waste of human life*, he thought.

The wind howled on. Dayton felt its icy fingers despite the fire. He sat up and rubbed his arms. The pain in his left forearm reminded him that the gash needed treatment. When the whiskey touched it, the fiery jolt took his breath. Blinking against the tears that rushed unbidden to his eyes, he rewound the crude bandage and slipped into his coat.

At some time in the middle of the night, while North Wind slept soundly and Dayton fought sleep, warming the soles of his boots by the fire, the wind stopped as abruptly as a door being slammed.

The sudden silence roused the Indian. He sat up, rubbing his eyes, and then turned them on the man who had saved his life. Observing Dayton's dull, sagging face, he said, "It is time for Chance Dayton to sleep. You take some of these coats. Wrap up and sleep. I am very warm and refreshed."

Dayton accepted the Indian's offer and promptly fell asleep. North Wind listened to the deathly silence and fed the fire as the hours passed. At the first light of dawn, the Indian rolled stiffly out of his bedroll and piled the last of the wood on the coals.

Dayton awakened to bright sunlight reflecting off the snow into his earthen shelter. He was perfectly warm, though the fire had burned out. To his surprise, he was buried beneath all the coats. . . . North Wind was gone.

Quickly, he crawled out into the gully, blinking against the sun's brilliance. The clear air was biting and cold. North Wind's tracks revealed that he had left the gully and headed west across the snow-laden prairie. But he was nowhere in sight. It was evident from his tracks that he was dragging his left leg.

Dayton returned to the shelter. The canvas sack was still there, and after inspecting its contents, he decided that North Wind had taken none of the food. Wanting to be on the move, he ate some cold jerky and headed west in the Indian's tracks. As the site of yesterday's battle came into view, he was pleased to see that both army and Indian horses, his own among them, had returned and congregated in the area.

North Wind had no doubt found his own horse and ridden for the Sioux camp. Realizing it would not be long until the Sioux came to claim their dead, Dayton knew he had to hurry.

One by one, the muscular man uncovered the frozen

bodies of the cavalrymen and tied them to the backs of the horses. Linking the bridles together with lengths of rope, Dayton formed a long train. Then he brushed snow from his own saddle and mounted his horse. It would be a two-day ride east to Fort Abraham Lincoln, but it was the only thing to do. From there he could wire Fort Keogh and inform the president of the stage company, William Thomas, that he would arrive in about five days.

At Fort Abraham Lincoln, two days later, the fifteen cavalrymen were buried at sunset with military honors. There was special lament over the loss of Colonel Albert Swain. The men of the fort had eagerly anticipated serving under the esteemed officer.

The next morning, Dayton wired William Thomas of his delay. He ate a hearty meal with Captain Edgar Gordon, the acting commandant, and left for Fort Keogh.

Several Oglala Sioux braves came rushing across the snow to greet North Wind as he rode into the camp. Others were busy digging a hole in the ground under the personal supervision of Black Claw himself. North Wind was surprised to see a young brave named Little Squirrel tied to a tree, his face blanched with fear.

Someone shouted, "It is North Wind!"

Black Claw turned and walked toward the spot where the men had halted North Wind's horse and were helping the brave to the ground. The solemn warrior chief eyed the bloody leg and then said, "The others?"

"All dead," replied North Wind in the Sioux tongue as he stood erect in the snow, but favoring his wounded leg.

Black Claw was a small man, standing less than five feet eight inches tall. He was slender but sinewy, and his skin was a light brown. He wore his full headdress, the colorful feathers waving slightly in the cold morning breeze, and around his neck, on the outside of the heavy buckskin coat, was his ever-present bear-claw necklace.

The chief placed a hand to his mouth and coughed. He was handed a flask by Angry Bear, his most trusted brave. The chief took a generous swig and coughed again. Handing the flask back to Angry Bear, he said, "North Wind will come to my tipi."

As North Wind limped behind Black Claw to the camp's largest shelter, Angry Bear called for Low Cloud, the medicine man.

Inside the tipi, Angry Bear sat beside Black Claw, who watched as Low Cloud removed the bloody strip of army shirt. The medicine man grunted. "What did you put on the wound?"

"Firewater," came North Wind's deep-voiced reply.

From a small fold of buffalo hide, Low Cloud produced a carefully wrapped piece of deer moss. He placed a wadded bunch on the wound, which still oozed blood, and wrapped it with a belt of deerskin. "Soon the pain will walk away," he said. "Deer moss will stop the bleeding and pull out the poison."

As Low Cloud left the tipi, Black Claw coughed; then he told Angry Bear to see to the digging of the hole. When he had gone, Black Claw said to North Wind, "Now tell me your story."

North Wind told the chief of the bloody battle that had taken place two days before, and he watched Black Claw's face register delight as he described, one by one, the deaths of the soldiers.

The sober chief looked at the empty sheath on the wounded warrior's belt. "North Wind left his knife in a bluecoat's body?"

"Yes."

"What about your hidden knife?"

"I still have it," responded North Wind.

Black Claw extended his open hand. For some reason he wanted to see the knife.

North Wind reached inside his buckskin shirt and

produced the small blade. The chief examined it closely, turning it from side to side. Meeting North Wind's gaze, he asked, "Were you the only survivor of the Oglala?"

"Yes."

"You must have killed the last bluecoat. But not with this knife. No blood is on this knife."

North Wind knew he must explain about Chance Dayton. There was suspicion lurking in Black Claw's dark eyes. "During the battle," he said, "a bullet struck my leg. I fell. Then—"

The explanation was interrupted by Angry Bear's face in the doorway. "The digging is finished," he said.

Black Claw spoke to his wounded brave. "I have an important matter to attend to now. I will hear the rest of your story later."

The chief moved outside, commanding North Wind to follow. All Oglala Sioux braves, he insisted, were to observe what was about to take place.

North Wind limped out to see that a fire had been built in the freshly dug pit, which measured two feet in width, four feet in length, and three feet in depth. Red and yellow flames danced from the heavy logs that were crisscrossed in the rectangular hole, and black billows of smoke lifted skyward.

A sharp command from Black Claw brought the entire camp of over fifty warriors to attention. North Wind saw two men untie Little Squirrel from the tree and lead him beside the blazing pit. Cold dread had frozen Little Squirrel's face into a mask of terror, his eyes riveted to the licking flames.

While the two braves held Little Squirrel by the arms, Black Claw moved close to the burning pit and motioned with his hands for the warriors to form a circle around him. A chill slithered down North Wind's spine as his gaze fell on the four stakes that had been driven into the ground. He had never seen a torture pit, but he had heard of them. The stakes were spaced so as to spread-eagle a man over the pit when his wrists and ankles were lashed to them. What on earth had Little Squirrel done to deserve this?

Two more logs were added to the fire as the chief lifted his palms. A deathly stillness settled over the camp. For a long moment, the only sounds were the crackling of the fire and Little Squirrel's shaky breathing.

Black Claw's face seemed to be chiseled from cold granite. Lifting his voice, he said, "I wish for every warrior to learn a valuable lesson this day. There is no greater crime for Oglala Sioux than treason. It is the *most* offensive!"

The chief's burning eyes were turned upon the trembling Indian who was held by strong hands. Pointing a stiff finger at him, Black Claw spewed out his accusation. "This man is a traitor!"

Little Squirrel shook his head fearfully, eyes bulging.

Black Claw told the entire camp of Little Squirrel's crime. On the previous day, the chief had sent a war party south to raid a white man's farm. His orders were to kill the entire family and burn the buildings. Angry Bear had led the party.

The chief succumbed to a spasm of coughing and then continued. His voice grew vehement as he revealed that Little Squirrel had shown compassion to a seven-year-old boy, making a pretense of killing the child, but then hiding him in an earth cellar to spare his life.

Black Claw's eyes grew wild and intense, and he stormed like a madman, the veins in his face and neck distended like corded rope. He roared that all whites, young or old, were enemies of the Sioux. Their lives were never to be spared. Any Oglala Sioux who did not take advantage of the opportunity to kill a white would be considered by Black Claw to be the white man's friend . . . and to be the white man's friend was to be Black Claw's enemy.

The enraged chief labeled Little Squirrel's conduct as

nothing short of treachery. Because of his evil deed, the traitor would be roasted to death, slowly, over the torture pit.

North Wind swallowed hard as the victim was stripped of his clothing and moved to the edge of the pit. Heat waves rose from its yawning mouth. The licking flames had died out, leaving behind them a bed of red-hot coals. North Wind's heart went out to Little Squirrel. He wondered if he would have killed the child had he been in Little Squirrel's shoes.

One thing he now felt certain of—he must not tell Black Claw about Chance Dayton. Black Claw would know that North Wind could have killed the white man and had not done so. He knew that North Wind had returned with the knife still strapped to his chest. North Wind's fate would be the same as Little Squirrel's, and as he thought about how close he had come to telling Black Claw about Chance Dayton, the brave's body quivered.

The chief broke in on North Wind's thoughts as he barked a command. Four braves flung Little Squirrel facedown over the smoldering pit, quickly securing his wrists and ankles to the stakes.

The blood-curdling screams cut the cold November air. Little Squirrel's torso was fully exposed to the scorching heat. As they looked on, the warriors, knowing they had to appear impassive, fought to maintain their composure. Black Claw was getting his message across: No Oglala Sioux was to show mercy to any white man.

The nauseating odor of burnt flesh filled the air as the ovenlike heat caused the skin to peel from Little Squirrel's body. The victim's raw screams seemed to reach the sky. North Wind wanted to turn away, but knew he dare not show the slightest sign of disgust for fear of being held up for ridicule among his peers. He had seen suffering, but nothing like this. His stomach began to protest.

Suddenly, a brave younger than North Wind wheeled

from the circle and darted for the trees, holding his hand over his mouth. He was quickly followed by another.

North Wind felt a cold sweat bead his brow, and his knees turned to water. Then Black Claw approached him and said, "You look pale, my brother. Let us return to my tipi, where you will be more comfortable."

Within moments, the two Indians were seated on the sod floor of the tipi, and Black Claw gave North Wind water to drink. As the warrior drank, the morose eyes of the chief settled on him. "I now wish to hear of the deaths of my warriors, and of North Wind's escape."

With Little Squirrel's weakening screams in the background, North Wind began to explain. "During the battle, a bullet struck my leg, and I fell. Then a soldier was standing over North Wind. He aimed his rifle, pulled at the trigger, but the gun was empty. The soldier hit me in head with the barrel, and I woke up much later. Everybody was dead."

It went against every fiber of North Wind's nature to lie. He had been taught by his father always to be truthful. "Truth is honorable," his father had often said. "To lie is a grievous shame. The Great Spirit looks down with a twisted face at a lie."

North Wind wondered if the Great Spirit did not look down with a twisted face at Little Squirrel's agony. He could barely hear the screaming now. His heart hurt for the lies he must tell, but he told himself that it was better to know pain in the heart than to experience what Little Squirrel was going through.

North Wind continued, "I found the soldier's firewater and poured it in the leg wound. Drank some, too. I took shelter for the night. This morning I found a horse and rode to camp."

Accepting his wounded warrior's story as truth, Black Claw asked about the location of the battle site. North Wind gave directions. Outside, Little Squirrel's cries had stopped. North Wind followed the chief out into the brilliant sunlight and listened as a detail was ordered to go to the site, round up the horses, and bring in the bodies. With venom in his voice, Black Claw told them to slit the throats of the soldiers and bring back every scalp.

North Wind limped to the center of the camp and watched with apprehension as the detail rode out. He thought of the tracks in the snow that would show a white man was still alive and would lead them straight to the shelter. By now, he hoped, Chance Dayton had left the scene. Possibly he had even gathered the horses and loaded up the bodies of the soldiers. If he had taken them east to Fort Abraham Lincoln, the trail to the shelter would be obliterated. The braves in the detail would figure the cavalry had simply picked up its dead, and they would think no more of it.

He prayed that there would be no trace of Chance Dayton. One word to Black Claw that contradicted his story, and North Wind was a dead man.

Chapter Three

A cold night wind swept over the broad Yellowstone River, flickering the flames in the lanterns along the main street of the bustling Montana Territory town of Fort Keogh, less than a half mile outside the stockade walls of the U.S. Army bastion that bore the same name.

Fort Keogh's citizens pulled up their coat collars against the chill as they moved along the wooden sidewalks. Low-burning night-lights glowed from glass store windows. The muffled sound of the tinkling saloon piano rode the gusty wind, growing louder when customers opened the door and went inside.

A tall, slender form emerged unnoticed from the darkness between two clapboard buildings and took up a position across the street from the Great Plains Overland Stage Company office. Leaning against a shop front in the deep shadows of its canopy, he flared a match, cupped it in his hands, and attempted to light the tip of his cigarillo.

The brisk wind stole the flame, and he swore under his breath and tried again. On the third attempt the cigarillo came alive, the smoke puffs instantly carried away into the night. With dark, vitriolic eyes, he studied the movements of the Great Plains agent inside the lit office across the street.

For a moment, the moon's half face appeared in the sky, lessening the darkness of the shadows. It was swallowed again by a thick bank of clouds, and the shadows of night deepened once more.

The tall man stiffened as Fred Meade, the Great Plains agent in Fort Keogh, stepped outside. Meade did not see the red tip of the cigarillo glowing in the darkness as his eyes swept the dimly lit street. He cocked an ear southward, looked at his pocket watch, shook his head, and started to go back inside. But before he had taken two steps, a horse's hooves sounded in the distance. He turned in the direction the horse seemed to be coming from and squinted into the deepening dusk. In a few moments he was able to make out the face of Chance Dayton, riding fast into town toward the stage-company office.

Dayton was greeted warmly by Meade and was ushered inside, where he removed his coat. Then he sat down and told his business associate about the battle with the Sioux. Explaining quickly that the post physician at Fort Abraham Lincoln had stitched up the gash in his arm, he asked when the coach from Cheyenne was due in. The coach was bringing stage-line president William Thomas, who would officiate at the inaugural ceremonies the day after tomorrow as the run to Fargo got under way.

"The dadburned thing's late already," Meade said, again pulling out his watch and checking the time. "Should've been here a good quarter of an hour ago. Doesn't look good for the president of the company to arrive late on one of his own coaches!" The stage agent laughed, pocketing his watch.

"I'll be over at the restaurant to grab a bite to eat," Dayton said as he rose. "You come get me if Mr. Thomas arrives."

"Sure thing, Chance," Meade said, extending his hand. "Good to have you back."

Dayton shook the agent's hand and, flinging his coat over his shoulder, walked out the door and headed for the restaurant. The sound of a tinkling piano grew louder as he neared a saloon, and the smell of cheap cigars and whiskey assailed his nostrils as he passed by its swinging doors.

A drunken cowboy stumbled past him as he continued down the wooden walkway toward the restaurant, a few doors beyond the saloon. The smell of food renewed his hunger, and he quickened his steps. Only a few customers remained this late, and Dayton was happy to give his order to the waitress immediately after he had entered and seated himself at a table. There would be no night life for him tonight, he reflected as his muscles relaxed and weariness fogged his brain. Tonight, a good night's sleep was all he wanted.

The wind had died down half an hour after Dayton's arrival when the rumbling hooves and the metallic tinkle of harnesses could be heard along the street. Again Fred Meade came out of the office, putting on a sheepskin jacket.

The four-horse team came to a stomping halt as the driver's voice boomed out, "Whoa!" The big Concord stagecoach rocked on its leather thoroughbraces and then settled.

"Howdy, Zeke!" Meade said. "You're a little late. What kept you?"

Zeke Hampton set the brake. "Was late leavin' Cheyenne to begin with. Mr. Thomas had some business to finish up there before we could pull out."

The shotgunner, Ted Gates, slid down and opened the coach door next to the boardwalk. "Just a few minutes, folks," he said, "and I'll have your luggage unloaded."

While Gates climbed up to the rack and began untying the ropes, the passengers emerged stiffly from the stagecoach. Fred Meade immediately stepped forth and gripped the hand of a stocky man in his early forties. "Sure glad to see you, Mr. Thomas!" he said as he vigorously pumped the arm of the Great Plains president. "Everything's ready to go here."

"Good!" responded Thomas. "Are Dayton and our driver, Jenkins, here?"

"Chance arrived about half an hour ago. He's having some dinner over at the restaurant. Jenkins wired me three days ago from Bozeman. He and his shotgunner will be here sometime tomorrow."

As Thomas and Meade continued their conversation, the townspeople began to gather to meet the passengers who planned to stay in the town of Fort Keogh. An elderly couple was met by a son and daughter-in-law. A middle-aged husband was greeted tearfully by his wife. A young mother held the hand of her four-year-old son, who was showing signs of wanting to run about after being cooped up in the stagecoach. She smiled at a youthful man who handed her a bundled baby, and said, "Thank you, Mr. Fleming. You've been such a help with Timmy and little Darlene. I don't know what I would have done without you."

Touching the brim of his hat and smiling in return, Mike Fleming said, "Ma'am, like I told you yesterday, I was mighty glad to help you with the young'uns. I'll get your luggage for you as soon as it comes off the rack."

As Fleming turned toward the coach, the boy wrenched his hand from his mother's grasp and ran up the boardwalk. Leaving Meade's side for a moment, the stage company president ran after the child and grabbed his arm. "Come on, Timmy," he said, smiling. "You stay with your mother."

Martha Dugan took Timmy's hand and scolded him. Then she said, "Thank you, Mr. Thomas. This boy is a handful." Smiling warmly, she added, "I want to compliment your company on its efficiency and friendliness. You have made the trip most pleasurable."

Fleming was taking Martha Dugan's two suitcases from the hands of the shotgunner when the final two passengers disembarked. Both were young women, but there the similarity ended. One seemed to sparkle with warmth and life—a petite blonde with friendly brown eyes and an upturned nose, her long hair coiled in ringlets in back with curls across her forehead—while the other, a tall, thin woman with straight, mousebrown hair, almost cowered behind her friend. The first woman seemed to greet life with eagerness and enthusiasm; the other acted as though she wanted to hide from it.

Neither of the women noticed the tall, slender form that detached itself from the deep shadows across the way and moved into the dim light of the street lamps. Pausing in the middle of the wagon-rutted street, the tall man shouted past the cigarillo clenched in his teeth, "*Fleming!*"

The bark of the man's voice was enough to quiet every person gathered around the stagecoach. One of the horses stamped and blew. A bay gelding tied to the hitching rail a few yards away nickered in return.

Martha Dugan's head came up. She pressed the baby to her breast and squeezed Timmy's hand hard with her own.

Fleming froze at the sound of the voice. He set the suitcases down and slowly stood erect. His features paled as he turned to face the man who stood in the street, two low-slung guns riding his narrow hips. Careful not to move his hands, he sucked in a nervous breath and exhaled the words, "I told you to leave me alone, Dakota!"

Fred Meade's voice met the ears of the clustered group in a half whisper. "*It's Dakota Smith!*"

A hush fell over the crowd. Though Dakota Smith

had never shown up in Fort Keogh before, everyone knew his reputation. All over the West men trembled at the mention of his name, for he was a cold-blooded murderer, and lightning with his guns.

In his sinister manner, the wiry young killer enjoyed intimidating his victims, watching them cower before him. Sneering through the smoke of his cigarillo, he said, "You're gonna draw against me, Fleming."

Holding his right hand far from the gun on his side, Mike Fleming answered, "I told you in Laramie that you'll not force me to draw against you. You're not going to make me do it. I'm no gunfighter."

"You should've thought of that when you smart-mouthed me in front of that woman," hissed the outlaw.

"She was more than a woman," Fleming rebutted. "She was a lady. All I did was ask you to quit using foul language in front of her."

Dakota Smith's face reddened. "Well . . . ain't you the big hero! Stalwart guardian of the ladies' ears! I should've forced a shoot-out then and there. The more I've thought about it, the madder it's made me. Nobody smart-mouths me and gets away with it."

"You'll have to gun me down in front of all these people," warned Fleming. "It'll be murder. I'm not drawing against you—"

"Why don't you go play gunfighter somewhere else?" William Thomas cut in, fixing the rawboned man with a look of irritation.

Dakota Smith whipped the cigarillo from his mouth and pointed its glowing tip at Thomas. "You shut up, mister, or you'll be next!"

"We'll see about that!" Thomas replied sharply, showing no fear of the deadly gunfighter.

Thomas wore no gun, and Dakota Smith told him to get one. While they argued, Fred Meade turned and whispered to one of the townspeople to go to the marshal's office. The man nodded and turned to leave the scene.

But the gunslinger saw the movement and barked, "Hey, you! Stay where you are!"

The man halted in his tracks.

Martha Dugan, fearing for her children's safety, started toward the office door along with the petite blond woman, Polly Temple, and her friend, Barbara Stevens.

"You, too, ladies!" snapped the tall man standing in the dim light of the street. "Stay right where you are!"

Martha froze, fear pinching her face. Polly's hand went to her mouth. Timmy, unaware of the danger, was struggling to free his hand from his mother's grip.

Dakota Smith turned his attention back to Mike Fleming. Unnoticed in an upstairs window, a woman was watching the incident. Hurriedly, she went down the back stairs and headed up the alley for the marshal's office.

"Now move out here in the street, Fleming," Dakota Smith said, sticking the cigarillo back in his mouth and rolling it from side to side in a cocky manner. "Quit sniveling like an old woman. Stand up and face me like a man!"

"I'll say it once more, Dakota," Fleming breathed. "I don't pretend to be a gunfighter. You'll not goad me into it. If you are going to kill me, it'll have to be cold-blooded murder."

Polly Temple swallowed hard, her heart clutched with icy fingers of fear. In a strangled voice, she said, "Why are you doing this? This good man is a gentleman. He corrected you for being crude. Is that any reason to kill him?"

With disgust, Fleming said, "Enough of this nonsense, Dakota." He started to turn, and the motion flared his coattails.

Dakota Smith whipped out his right-hand gun and fired. The flat roar of the gun echoed and reverberated among the clapboard facades of the buildings along the street. Two women screamed as Mike Fleming fell in a heap.

The stunned onlookers stood like statues in disbelief. The piano stopped playing in the saloon down the street, and faces appeared at windows along the boardwalk.

The killer gave the wide-eyed crowd a cynical look as he holstered the weapon.

"You murderer!" Polly Temple shrieked.

At the same instant, swift footsteps were heard, followed by the appearance of Fort Keogh's young deputy, Jim Chapman. The tall, lean deputy glanced at the man on the ground and then eyed Dakota Smith. "What happened here?" he demanded.

Martha Dugan was losing her grip on Timmy as Dakota Smith coldly replied, "The man drew on me."

"That's a lie!" Thomas spoke up. "Take a look, Deputy. The gun is still in his holster."

Fleming's holstered gun was in plain view. Chapman pulled his eyes from it, back to the killer's shadowed face. "What do you mean, he *drew* on you?"

"What I meant was, he *started* to," Dakota Smith said. "I had to shoot him to defend myself. You can't fault me for that."

"He's Dakota Smith, Jim," Fred Meade said.

The deputy's face stiffened as he pulled his gun and leveled it on the killer. Dakota Smith made no move toward the pearl-handled Colts thonged to his thighs. "You're under arrest!" Chapman snapped.

"Now, just a minute, mister," the outlaw said. "The man was going for his gun. Is it my fault if he was slow?"

"He's lying, Deputy," Thomas said. "Take a look where the bullet hit him."

As Deputy Jim Chapman moved toward the lifeless form on the ground, Martha Dugan shifted the position of the baby in her arms and then gripped Timmy's hand again.

The crowd watched as Chapman, holding his gun on the tall man, carefully knelt beside Mike Fleming's body. His eyes moving cautiously between the fallen

40

man and the outlaw, he located the bullet hole. The slug had entered Fleming's back at an angle, just below the right arm.

The muzzle of his gun still leveled on the killer, Chapman rose and said in a steady voice, "I never saw a man go into a gunfight backwards. Like I said, you're under arrest. For murder."

Dakota Smith bristled, arching his back. "You ain't jailin' me," he snarled.

Ted Gates stood by Zeke Hampton and wished for the twelve-gauge that lay up in the box. Chapman was going to need help.

"Hold that gun on him steady, Jim," Gates spoke up, heading toward the coach. "I'll get my shotgun. Then we'll pull his claws."

At that instant, Timmy Dugan slipped his hand from his mother's grip and darted innocently toward the street, running between Dakota Smith and Chapman. Martha screamed at him helplessly, but before the child could react, Dakota Smith's hands moved down toward his gunbelt. He saw hesitation in the deputy's eyes—to fire would endanger the child—and then, with no regard for Timmy, the killer drew both guns and fired. They blossomed orange in the dim light, the sound of the blast rocketing against the buildings.

The impact of the slugs flattened Chapman on his back instantly. Timmy, frightened by the loud noise, stumbled and fell in the street, while Martha held back the panic rising in her throat and Thomas restrained her from dashing into the line of fire with her baby.

Ted Gates had reached the box and was bringing up the twelve-gauge when Dakota Smith swung his guns and fired. The shotgunner slumped over the rack, dead.

Instantly, the yellow-haired killer holstered one gun and seized the boy by the arm. Holding the other gun on the crowd, he slowly backed toward the dark area between the two buildings where he had first appeared

41

on the street. While retreating, he said, "Anyone tries to stop me, I'll kill this brat!"

Timmy wailed and called his mother, and Martha screamed, "Please! Don't take my boy! Please!"

At that moment Chance Dayton appeared at the edge of the crowd, which stood transfixed by what was taking place. He saw that the deputy and Mike Fleming were shot, and he started to move toward them. But when he glanced to where Timmy's screams were coming from and saw that the outlaw was holding the boy hostage, he halted, not wanting to endanger the boy's life. His heart pounded with rage as he watched the man and boy disappear into the darkness between the buildings. Timmy's crying could still be heard when they were out of sight.

Dayton heard a moan and looked to where Jim Chapman lay in the street. The deputy rolled over, and Dayton and the stage driver moved toward him. Chapman had a bullet in his chest and another in his shoulder. Groggily, he raised himself up on his knees.

At that moment Dakota Smith reappeared on horseback from between the buildings, with Timmy seated in the saddle in front of him. Guiding the horse toward Chapman, he waved Dayton and the driver away with his gun. They had no choice but to back off, and as they did, Dakota Smith aimed the muzzle at the swaying deputy's head and squeezed the trigger. Chapman died instantly, the bullet ripping into his skull.

The small crowd stood in numb terror as the youthful killer shouted, "Anybody tries to follow me gets the same thing!"

He spun the horse around, and Martha Dugan reached a trembling hand in the direction of her terrified little son. No sound escaped her lips as her throat constricted with shock.

Then Dakota Smith spurred his mount. Man, boy, and horse were instantly swallowed by the night.

* * *

As soon as Dakota Smith and his young hostage were gone, Chance Dayton lifted Jim Chapman's lifeless body and carried him into the stage office, instructing two men to follow with the other victims. Polly Temple had taken hold of the frantic mother, and to her brown-haired friend she said, "Please, Barbara, will you take the baby?" Turning to Martha, she said, "Let's go into the stage office, Martha."

"My son!" Martha exclaimed, sobbing. "He's got my son!"

"Everything's going to be all right," the blond-haired woman said. "Come on with me, Martha." She led the weeping woman up the steps, and the door was opened by Sarah Meade, the wife of Fort Keogh's stage agent.

Dayton and the other men were already in the office, having placed the dead bodies in a back room. The ex-cavalry officer stopped as he saw the women enter. Then he walked up to Polly and said, "Ma'am, my name is Chance Dayton. I'm going after the boy right now, and you can be sure I'm not going to let anything happen to him. You just stay here and try to calm his mother."

The woman looked at Dayton with grateful eyes and extended her hand. "Mr. Dayton, I'm Polly Temple. God bless you for your help. We'll be waiting for you to return with the child. Thank you."

As he shook her soft hand, Dayton thought he had never seen a woman so beautiful, and he felt his knees go weak. But a sob from the distraught mother brought back to him the urgency of his quest, and he turned toward the door.

Martha Dugan allowed herself to be seated by Polly and Sarah. Barbara sat nearby with the baby.

"I'm going with you, Chance," William Thomas said as he appeared at the door.

"William! Glad you're here. I'll need your help,"

Dayton said. "We'd better get started. Are there horses we can use?"

"I saw a couple outside," the stage company president replied.

"Let's go, then," Dayton said, and he looked back at the women, his eyes lingering on those of Polly Temple for a moment.

Polly accompanied them to the door and then returned to where Martha sat. "Everything will be all right," she repeated softly. "They'll be back with your son."

Martha nodded, still unable to speak, fear clouding her eyes.

The saloon had emptied out, and people had emerged from other buildings and were clustered around the stage office. The driver was up on the stagecoach attending to the body of Ted Gates, the shotgunner, and eyewitnesses were telling newcomers of Dakota Smith's young hostage.

Quieting the crowd, Thomas asked if someone would lend him and Dayton horses. A man stepped forward, pointed toward the hitching rail, and said, "That's my horse right there, mister. You're welcome to him."

Another man stepped forward and said, "Mine's the bay. He's all yours. But we ought to get up a posse to go after Dakota."

"Right now the main thing is the little boy," Dayton said. "I think Dakota Smith will dump him before he goes too far. Timmy will only slow him down." With that, he dashed to the horse, loosened the reins from the rail, and leaped into the saddle, while Thomas mounted the other horse.

One of the men in the crowd shouted, "C'mon, boys! Let's get our guns and go with 'em!"

"No!" Dayton called out. "It's better that we go alone. Our main concern right now is Timmy Dugan. If Dakota hasn't released him yet and sees only two men on his trail, he'll probably let the boy go, to slow us down. If he sees a whole posse, he may use the boy as a shield. Let's hold off the posse until we're sure Timmy is safe."

"Okay, mister," came the voice of the same man. "You seem to know what you're doin'."

While the horse chomped at the bit, sensing he was in for a good run, Dayton looked into their faces and said, "I see that young man was your deputy. Where's your marshal?"

"He's up in Rock Springs," replied another man. "Town about thirty-five miles north of here. He's due back tomorrow."

Dayton nodded and then dug his heels into the animal's ribs. Thomas spurred his mount, too, and within seconds the two men vanished into the darkness.

The town's physician appeared on the scene with black bag in hand, but he soon realized that his services were not needed. Instead, the undertaker was summoned and the bodies were carried away.

Ralph Eberling, chairman of the town council, watched the men move away with the bodies. The stage driver was weeping as he helped carry the lifeless form of his partner. When they passed from view, Eberling entered the Great Plains office. Fred Meade stood looking on as Polly talked soothingly to Martha Dugan while Barbara held the baby.

Slowly, Martha found her voice and explained to the women that her father owned a ranch some twenty miles northwest of town. She was to spend the night in the nearby hotel, and her parents were to come for her and the children tomorrow morning.

"Well, honey," Sarah Meade said, "let's take you and the baby on over to the hotel, and—"

"No!" cut in the distraught mother. "I'm going to stay right here until Mr. Dayton comes back."

"All right, all right," Polly said, patting Martha's hand. "We'll wait right here."

Eberling and Meade moved into the inner office and closed the door. As they sat down, Eberling said, "That man said his name is Dayton?"

"Chance Dayton. He's an agent of the stage company. He's the one who set up the new route between here and Fargo. The other man, Thomas, oversees the whole operation. He's here to conduct the ceremony for the opening of the new route."

Several heavy footsteps were heard in the outer office. Meade rose from his chair and opened the door. Some of the townsmen, along with the stage driver, had returned to wait for Dayton and Thomas. All were concerned about the child.

Motioning from the door, Meade said, "Why don't you men come on in here? Leave the ladies alone with Mrs. Dugan."

As the men crowded into the small office, Meade clapped a hand on the driver's shoulder and said, "Zeke, I'm sorry about Ted."

Zeke Hampton shook his head, saying with quivering lips, "Best partner I ever had, Fred."

One of the other men spoke up and said, "There'll be the devil to pay when the marshal gets back. Bad enough the shotgun guard and that Fleming fellow bein' killed like they were, but Jim Chapman is somethin' altogether different. He was like a son to Marshal Banner."

"Yes, sir, that's the truth," Meade affirmed. "Banner had found in Jim what his wife had taken from him nigh on twenty years ago."

"Logan Banner was married?" Damon Woods, the town barber, asked incredulously.

"Sure was," Meade answered. "Her name was Lee Ann. A pretty girl she was, and blond as Banner. They had a boy name of Lindsey. Spittin' image of his father. Well, Lee Ann, she took up with a gambler who came

46

to town when the boy was, oh, eight or nine. Ran away with the man—his name was Duane Vivian. Kind of sissy name for a gambler, I always thought. Anyway, she took the boy with her, and Banner's never seen him since."

A man named Charlie Tack said, "All this time I never knew that about the marshal. . . . When did Jim Chapman become his deputy?"

Eberling answered, "Five years ago. Chapman came here from Minnesota, and the marshal kind of helped him along. The lad seemed to give Banner a new outlook on life."

"Whew!" Tack exclaimed. "I wouldn't want to be in that Dakota Smith's boots with Logan Banner on my tail! Banner will be after him with blood in his eye!"

Eberling rubbed his chin, nodding in agreement. "Dakota Smith might as well carve his name on his grave marker. He's a dead man."

Tack looked at the Great Plains agent and said, "Fred, that killer's name ain't really *Smith*, is it?"

"Nope," responded Meade.

"It ain't?" Hampton asked, eyebrows arched.

Meade shook his head. "First name isn't Dakota, either."

"How do you know?" Eberling queried.

"There's a report on him over in Banner's office," Meade explained. "The report was sent to lawmen all over these parts. I read it through. Not only that, but I talked to a man who saw the kid in action. Seems this young feller was in a Fargo saloon one night about ten years ago—I think it was called the Yellow Rose. The bartender refused to serve him, saying the kid was too young. He grabbed the bartender and put a gun between his eyes. Said he was old enough, and the bullet would blow the bartender's brains out even if a two-year-old pulled the trigger!"

"Bet he got his drink, huh?" asked one of the men.

"Yeah," Meade said. "That's not all. He also got the

attention of one of the dance-hall girls. Her name was Jamie Lynn something. Can't think of her last name. Anyway, the kid took a bottle and a glass to a table, and this girl sat down and started talking to him. Said she liked a man that had guts and could handle himself. Pretty soon, in walks Clay Boswell."

"*Clay Boswell?*" echoed Charlie Tack. "Now, you ain't gonna tell us it was this Dakota Smith kid that took out Clay Boswell?"

"Sure was," Meade said.

Tack gave a low whistle. "Clay Boswell was one of the fastest guns around!"

"*Was* is right," said Meade. "But you've got me ahead of my story. Clay Boswell was sweet on this Jamie Lynn. He saw red when he eyed Dakota Smith and her snuggled up close at the table. He walked right up and told Jamie Lynn to get away from him. Well, she had already seen her new friend handle the bartender and was eager to see him up against the likes of Clay Boswell, so she egged him on by asking the kid to make Boswell go away."

"Did the kid realize who he was dealin' with?" Hampton asked.

"I'm just coming to that," Meade said, enjoying his eager audience.

"At this point, Boswell said to the kid, 'I'm Clay Boswell. Now who might *you* be?' Trying to buffalo the youngster with his famous name. But the kid just eyed him coldly and said, 'You can call me Mr. Smith.'"

"Like he wasn't gonna tell his real name, eh?" put in Charlie Tack.

"That's the way it added up to me," Meade affirmed. "So the girl pushed it further, and those two fellers got into it. The kid just plain outdrew Boswell and dropped him dead in his boots. Far as anybody knows, the kid had never been in a gunfight before, but he'd sure enough been practicing his fast draw. The report says he got a taste for gun smoke and blood right there, and he's been killing ever since. For lack of knowing his real name, the law and the public call him Dakota Smith."

One of the group said, "Fred, how did you know it was Dakota Smith who was challengin' that Fleming fellow out there in the street?"

"From the report in Logan Banner's office."

"Were there pictures?"

"No pictures," replied Meade. "Just a detailed description. Said he was over six feet tall . . . skinny . . . yellow hair. When Fleming called him 'Dakota,' I took one look and knew it was him. Couldn't see his face real well, but everything else fit the description."

"How many men has he killed?" Damon Woods asked.

"Law doesn't know. But he's had ten years of shedding blood from the Dakotas to New Mexico, Kansas to Arizona. Returns to Fargo periodically, report says, to see that Jamie Lynn hussy. Probably where he's headed now."

"Well, if they know he keeps showing up in Fargo," queried Woods, "why don't they set a trap and catch him?"

Meade smiled wryly. "They tried it twice. Total of three lawmen have died. Marshal in Fargo trembles in his boots when Dakota Smith rides into town . . . just looks the other way. Can't say as I blame him."

Ralph Eberling drew a deep breath and let it out slowly. "Might end up like Jim Chapman otherwise."

"Yeah." Meade nodded. "No wonder that Fleming feller was scared."

The stage driver shook his head. "Poor ol' Ted. He never should have gone up there after that shotgun. Didn't stand a chance." Zeke sniffed and ran the back of his hand under his nose.

An elderly man in the group scratched at his three-day growth of beard and said with a cracked voice, "Well, that dadburned Dakota Smith done fixed hisself this time. There ain't no lawman like Logan Banner."

"Especially when he's mad," added another.

"Yeah," Eberling agreed. "And when Banner sees Jim's dead body, he's gonna be madder'n a teased diamondback!"

Meade stood up and walked to the door. Pulling it open, he eyed the four women in the outer office. Barbara Stevens was changing the baby's diaper while Polly sat with Martha, who was wringing her hands. She was no longer weeping. Addressing his wife, who was standing at the window, Fred asked, "How are things going?"

Sarah tried to smile. "As well as can be expected."

Anger rioted in Dayton's head as the powerful animal beneath him plunged through the darkness in front of the horse of William Thomas. Thinking of the dead men back in town, Dayton remembered that Dakota Smith had been in Denver about a year ago and had been involved in a shoot-out that had left dead two men and an eleven-year-old boy, who had been hit by a stray bullet.

Now the ruthless killer had taken hostage a four-year-old. According to what William Thomas had told him, the child could have been killed back there in town—the gunman had let bullets fly in spite of the boy's being in the line of fire. And Timmy's dangerous position had cost the young deputy marshal his life.

The two Great Plains men followed the road, heading due east, the direction Dakota Smith had taken. Little by little, the clouds dissipated, allowing the half moon to shower a spray of silver light on the plains.

Dayton pushed his horse at top speed, praying that Dakota Smith would stop and leave the child behind unharmed. As the wind whistled in his ears, he felt a chill wash over his body . . . not from the cold November air but from the thought that the killer could easily ambush them. There were trees, gullies, and heavy clumps of brush in abundance. Any of them would provide the outlaw with sufficient cover to cut him and Thomas down.

But Dayton rode on despite his fears. Suddenly, he saw movement on the road ahead of him. He called back to Thomas and pulled his horse to a halt. Standing in the stirrups, he squinted against the pale light. For a few seconds he thought his eyes had played a trick on him. Then he saw it: A dark object was quickly pulling behind the edge of a rock face in the distance. "That's Dakota," he said to Thomas, then raked his horse's ribs with his heels. Thomas followed, and after three minutes, they saw Timmy Dugan in the middle of the road ahead. The child was walking in a wide circle, frightened and whimpering.

At first, the disoriented boy thought the killer had come back for him, and he began to cry out.

Leaping from the saddle, Dayton said, "Don't cry, son. We've come to take you to your mother."

Timmy's fears subsided at the sound of the kind voice. The tall, dark-haired man gathered him up in his arms and held him tight until the weeping stopped. Still holding the boy, Dayton said to Thomas, "Timmy needs to go back to his mother right away, William. Will you take him? I'd like to go after Dakota Smith. He can't be too far ahead, and the sooner I get on his trail again, the better my chances of finding him."

"I'll be glad to take the boy back, Chance, but are you sure you want to go after that killer alone?"

"I'll be fine, William. I hope to be back at Fort Keogh with Dakota Smith before the inaugural run the day after tomorrow," Dayton said with a smile.

Thomas swung up in the saddle, and Dayton handed the boy over to him, placing him to the front of the stage-company president. "Are you ready to ride back to town?" Thomas asked, pulling the small body close.

Martha Dugan's son looked up and smiled at Thomas

in the moonlight, the fear gone from his tiny face. "Can we go as fast as that bad man did?"

The Great Plains president chuckled. "We can sure try, little partner."

Fred Meade paused in the doorway of the stage office and said, "Sarah, how about fixing up a pot of coffee? Might help Mrs. Dugan. The rest of us could use some, too. This vigil might last awhile."

"Good idea," Sarah agreed. Turning to the three women, she said, "Let's go upstairs. We can talk in the kitchen while the coffee brews."

The agent watched the women start up the stairs and then wheeled back to the men gathered in the office. "Poor little gal," he said, wagging his head.

"One thing Banner will have to do," Eberling said, "is get this town another deputy before he lights out after that killer."

"That's for sure," Damon Woods added. "He can't go off and leave this town without a lawman."

"Even if we get one, outlaws in these parts will start comin' into town if Marshal Banner is gone for very long."

The group agreed and laughed about the imaginary signs that could have been posted at both ends of town and that would have read *Notice to all outlaws, gunslingers, and riffraff. Logan Banner is marshal here!*

The sound of heavy footsteps in the outer office cut off their laughter. As the men were finding their feet, William Thomas stepped through the door, his face in a broad smile as he held Timmy Dugan in his arms. The boy said, "Where's my mommy?"

Meade whirled and dashed to the foot of the stairs. Cupping his hands to his mouth, he shouted exuberantly, "Mrs. Dugan! Mrs. Dugan! Timmy's back! Mr. Thomas found him. He's all right!"

Turning back to Thomas, Meade asked, "Where's Chance?"

"He insisted on going on after Dakota Smith," Thomas answered. "I hope he'll be all right."

After a tearful reunion with her little son, Martha thanked Thomas heartily for his deed and left for the hotel. Polly and Barbara went with her. The townsmen headed for their homes, speaking in low tones of Dayton's bravery—and the wrath of Logan Banner that would fall on Dakota Smith.

Once they were alone, Thomas and Meade sat down in the inner office, each sipping on a cup of steaming coffee.

"I hope we can get that stagecoach out of here as planned, on the twenty-fifth. That's only two days from now."

"Chance is one dependable hombre," said Meade. "You know his reputation. If at all possible, he'll be back here in time."

"Is everything else ready?"

"Yes, sir. We've got plenty of red ribbon, and the band members have been practicing. That brand-new Concord is all cleaned and polished."

"Excellent!" remarked Thomas.

With delight, the two men discussed the new stagecoach route between Fort Keogh and Fargo. Thomas figured that by late spring or early summer, his company would have six coaches running the route simultaneously.

"I think it's good that Chance will be riding the stage on the inaugural journey," Meade commented.

"We hired Chance for the job of pioneering these new routes because of his aggressiveness and his ability as a troubleshooter," Thomas said. "He's tough and resourceful. His military background is responsible for that, I suppose. Anyway, he'll be a good stabilizer for Jenkins and Hillyer. Drivers and shotgunners are always a little edgy on the first run."

Meade sipped his coffee and said, "Of course, those two are no greenhorns."

"Both veterans," Thomas agreed. "They've worked together as a team since the first time Wells Fargo ran a stagecoach in California. We wanted them on the Fargo route because of its length . . . and because of the potential Indian trouble."

Meade drained his cup and stood up. "Well, like I told you earlier, Jenkins wired me from Bozeman. He and Hillyer will be here tomorrow. As for Chance, I wouldn't lose any sleep. He'll be back here in time— and with Dakota Smith in tow, barring a blizzard or a couple thousand Sioux. Four or five hundred of them wouldn't slow him down much."

William Thomas laughed. "There's probably more truth than fiction in that statement."

Chapter Four

The sun was at its peak in the blue winter sky as Marshal Logan Banner rode into Fort Keogh the following day. As he headed up the main street, one of the town's citizens waved at him from the porch of a house and then quickly turned around and went inside, not wanting to be the one to tell the gray-haired marshal of Jim Chapman's death.

No one wanted that task.

Logan Banner was a tall, slender man in his early fifties. Rawhide tough and short on temper, his reputation caused most outlaw troublemakers to detour around his domain. The imaginary signs at the ends of town that the people joked about were as effective as if they were real. The bodies of several skeptics lay in the nearby graveyard as proof.

As Banner continued his ride through the town, he began to sense that something was askew. Citizens ordinarily warm and talkative avoided him as he rode up the street. *No doubt Jim will have the answer*, he told himself.

Dismounting in front of his office, the marshal strode stiffly across the wooden walkway. Turning the doorknob, he was surprised to find it locked. He pulled the pocket watch from his vest and saw that it was just past noon. Jim would be at the Sunshine Café. He then remembered his own empty stomach and decided to take his horse across the street to the livery stable and meet Jim at the café.

As Banner led his mount through the gate at the livery, the hostler saw him coming and was suddenly nervous. "Just leave him right there, Marshal," he said, backtracking. "I'll unsaddle him for you. Right now, I gotta leave. Won't be gone long."

With that, the hostler disappeared. Looking puzzled, Banner returned to the boardwalk. As he walked toward the café, a wagon came along. He recognized Clyde and Evelyn Perkins, both heavy talkers. Expecting Clyde to stop for a chat, Banner angled toward the street. But when Perkins spotted the marshal, he looked quickly at his wife and then back at Banner, and said, "Howdy, Marshal!" and kept on going.

At that, Fort Keogh's marshal decided to get to the bottom of this mystery. When he removed his hat and entered the Sunshine Café seconds later, the place was a hive of activity. There were a few strange faces, but he knew almost everyone. Standing near the door for a moment, he looked around for his deputy.

As the patrons of the café became aware of Banner's presence, conversation dropped markedly, enough for the marshal to notice. Not finding Jim Chapman, he walked toward Ralph Eberling's table.

The chairman of Fort Keogh's town council ran a nervous palm over his face as Banner threaded his way among the tables. Forcing a smile, Eberling said, "Hello, Logan. You . . . ah . . . just ride in?"

"Yeah," nodded the rawboned man. "I'm looking for Jim. Know where I might find him?"

Eberling's face lost its color. "Well, I, uh . . ."

"What's going on here, Ralph?" Banner demanded.

"Everybody in this town sees me and runs the other way. Have I got the plague, or something?"

Eberling knew the repugnant job of informing the marshal of Jim Chapman's death had fallen on him. Standing up, his meal half eaten, he said, "Let's go over to your office, Logan."

Nodding toward the table, Banner said, "You haven't finished your lunch. We can talk here."

Eberling shook his head. "I'm really not hungry, Logan. Come on. Let's go."

The two men left the restaurant, stepped off the boardwalk, and angled for the marshal's office. Though pressed to make conversation, Eberling evaded revealing the truth until the door was unlocked and they were inside.

"All right," Banner said. "Out with it. What's going on here? Where's Jim?"

Eberling took a deep breath, pursed his lips, and as if it burned his tongue to say the words, slowly said, "Jim's dead, Logan."

The office was instantly like a crypt. To Marshal Logan Banner, Eberling's words seemed unreal and strangely remote, like distant thunder. It seemed to be someone else's voice when he heard himself say, "Dead? My deputy is *dead*?"

Eberling nodded and reached for a chair.

Banner seized the man's arm, squeezing hard. "What happened? Who killed him?"

Wincing, Eberling said, "Sit down, Logan, and I'll tell you."

Like a sleepwalker, the stunned lawman rounded the corner of his desk and slumped into the chair. He removed his hat and laid it on the desk. Squaring his jaw, he asked, "Who? How?"

"Dakota Smith."

"*Dakota?*" Banner roared, and instantly rose to his feet, swearing loud enough for those outside on the street to hear his angry, booming voice. He paced the office like a caged lion while Eberling told him the story. The head of the town council was careful to explain that Jim had taken the first two bullets because he would not fire his gun with the boy between himself and the outlaw.

Banner became uncontrollable again when he heard how the cold-blooded killer had ended Chapman's life with a third bullet in the head. After a blast of profanity, Banner cooled slowly and listened to Eberling tell of the deaths of Mike Fleming and Ted Gates.

Sitting once again in the chair behind his desk, the marshal fought the tears that were scalding his eyes. "Ralph," he said, lower lip quivering, "I'm sorry about those other two men. But Jim . . . was like a son to me. I mean, I loved him like I would love my own son, Ralph."

The chairman of the town council thought back to what Meade had said about Banner's wife leaving him and taking their son with her. Now the old wound had been reopened. Logan had adopted Jim Chapman in his heart, but even his adopted son had been taken from him.

The marshal's grief was once again overcome by his blazing fury. The blood drained from his face and left it pallid. Breathing through clenched teeth, he hissed, "I'm going after him, Ralph. Dakota Smith—or whatever his name is—will answer to me! This earth isn't big enough to hide him. I'll get him if I have to follow him to hell itself!"

"Logan," Eberling said, forcing steadiness into his voice, "remember you are a lawman. Don't become vindictive. Your jurisdiction ends at the outskirts of town. It'll take a federal marshal—"

"Federal marshal!" he bellowed. "*I* am going after him, Ralph! He shed blood in my town. He murdered my deputy! He's mine, Ralph. *Mine!* I just hope Chance Dayton hasn't found him yet."

The marshal's entire body trembled with fury. All

morning Eberling had dreaded this reaction. A flea would come closer to stopping an elephant than any man would come to stopping Logan Banner. And with Dayton after Dakota Smith as well, the outlaw was a dead man. It was like Eberling himself had said the other night: *Dakota Smith might as well carve his name on his grave marker.*

Logan Banner knew a man who lived on a ranch just outside of town who was looking for a permanent job as deputy marshal. Judd Workman had filled in for Jim Chapman several times and had always done a competent job. Banner sent a messenger out to the ranch and got back word that Workman would arrive that evening, leaving Banner free to look for Dakota Smith.

The vengeful marshal met with stage-line president William Thomas that same afternoon. Thomas explained that he had decided to delay the inaugural run until Chance Dayton returned, which might not be until Dakota Smith was brought to justice. Banner nodded cordially, but his mind was elsewhere. His interest lay in joining Dayton on the trail of the yellow-haired killer who called himself Dakota Smith.

After leaving Thomas, the marshal went back to the café and forced himself to have a solid meal. He hadn't eaten all day, and he needed his strength to go after Jim Chapman's killer and to see justice done for Mike Fleming and Ted Gates.

Late that afternoon, Marshal Logan Banner rode out of Fort Keogh, his face set flint-hard as he headed due east. He figured Dakota Smith was on his way to Fargo. According to the reports on his desk, it seemed the outlaw could not stay away from Jamie Lynn Hargrove too long at a time.

The broad prairie was mantled in an icy crust of windswept snow as Chance Dayton rode eastward beyond

Baker, near the Dakota Territory border. It was now the second day after setting out from Fort Keogh on the trail of Dakota Smith. For the past three hours he had been following the north bank of a small, half-frozen stream. The tall cottonwood trees that lined its banks stood leafless against the crystal sky, and the late-afternoon sun glared off the snow, causing him to ride with eyes slitted against the white brilliance.

The ex-cavalry officer seemed like a beast of prey that had the fresh scent of its victim in its nostrils. He knew now that Dakota Smith was not far ahead of him. Residents of Baker had informed him that the arrogant killer had hung around town for a while, getting drunk and playing poker. They said he had boasted of gunning down a lawman in Fort Keogh and wished aloud that Baker had one so he could kill him, too. That same morning, the outlaw had goaded a young rancher into drawing against him. The rancher, somewhat clumsy with his sidearm, had died in the smoke of the killer's guns.

Dayton marveled at Dakota Smith's brazen insolence toward the law. It was as if he thought no one would be on his trail. Or else he was defying them to catch up to him, bragging of the slaughter he had left behind.

Well, you hang on, Mr. Dakota Smith, thought Dayton. *I'm coming. And I'm not far behind.*

As Dayton rode on, the steady sound of the horse's hooves crunching snow recalled the winter days of his boyhood in Columbus, Ohio. His mind flashed back to his youth, and the face of Lily Andrews appeared vividly before him. Releasing a heavy sigh that struck the cold air and plumed into a hazy vapor, he fought to no avail the haunting memories that stung his heart like angry hornets.

As so many times before, he relived those childhood days that he had shared with the lovely daughter of a lawyer. When the last year of high school had passed, the two had talked seriously of their future together.

Dayton would get his college degree, and then they would be married.

During his first year of college, the Civil War broke out. President Lincoln issued a plea for able-bodied men to join the army and help end the conflict with the Confederate states. Young Dayton left school to sign up. On the day of his departure, Lily kissed him tenderly and said, "I'm so proud of you, Chance. Take care of yourself, and come back to me. I love you so."

The tip of his tongue ran lightly over his lips as he remembered that final kiss. Through nearly four years of bloody battles, often facing death, that kiss and her plea to come back had kept him strong.

Bitterness surged through the broad-shouldered man as he rode on, remembering that warm day in May of 1865 when he had returned home to Lily. . . .

The big engine had chugged to a stop in front of the depot in downtown Columbus. The war was over, and he had come back to the girl he loved. Grabbing his small bag, young Dayton had peered momentarily through the dirty, flyspecked window of the railroad car. Many eager faces had lined the platform—but there was no sign of Lily. The crowd was large, though. She was out there, all right.

As he waited in line, filing slowly behind what seemed like a multitude of blue uniforms, he thought of her last kiss . . . her soft voice . . . the promise of love in her eyes. His heart throbbed with anticipation as he left the car and stepped onto the platform. Wives, sweethearts, parents, and friends were tearfully greeting the men in blue.

Dayton's dark-brown eyes searched the crowd. Where was Lily? Certainly she had received his letters. No one else could be there to meet him. Both parents had died of influenza when he was a child. His older sister had finished raising him, but she and her family had moved to Illinois.

Young Dayton felt intense disappointment when he

finally left the depot to walk to Lily's house. Certainly there was some reason. . . .

A buggy came bounding up the street. As it slowed, the driver began waving, calling, "Chance! Chance!"

Dayton recognized the face of Morton Pugmire. He was a man in his midforties and quite wealthy, having received a huge inheritance from his departed father, including Columbus's largest clothing store.

As the merchant drew up to the sidewalk, Dayton smiled and said, "Hello, Mr. Pugmire."

It was immediately evident that Pugmire was nervous and on edge. Climbing from the buggy, the flabby, pot-bellied man said, "Chance, I'm glad to see that you're all in one piece. Some of the boys—"

"I know," young Dayton cut in. "War is brutal."

Running a shaky hand over his thick lips, Pugmire said, "Chance, I, uh . . . need to talk to you."

"To me?" asked the man in blue, lifting his eyebrows. "About what?"

"Lily," came the blunt answer.

"Lily?"

"She received your letters, Chance, but . . . well, she doesn't want to see you."

Dayton's war-weary face tightened. His eyes honed to black points of puzzlement. "What do you mean, she doesn't want to see me? Has something happened to her? Has—"

"She's married, Chance," was Pugmire's cold retort.

The words seemed to strike Chance Dayton's ears like red-hot irons. "*Married?*" he echoed. "To whom?"

Pugmire sucked in a deep breath, squaring his shoulders. "To me."

Dayton could not believe what he was hearing. Why would Lily, young, beautiful Lily, marry a short, fat, forty-year-old, rich . . . *rich*. Was that it? Anger was claiming him as he said, "Well, we will just see about that! I'll talk to her, and—"

"Talking won't help, Chance," Pugmire said, gaining

courage. "There are children. Two of them. We're all very happy. Go away and . . . and please don't bother us."

Dayton's blood flared hot, and anger swelled his veins. He had a sudden insatiable desire to crush . . . to destroy. The bag in his hand dropped to the sidewalk, and a rock-hard fist slammed into Pugmire's fleshy jaw. The man went down like a rotten tree in a high wind. He was still on the ground when Dayton picked up his bag, looked over his shoulder, and reentered the depot. . . .

After that he had gone to Kansas City. He had not been looking for anything in particular when the job with Wells Fargo had opened up.

After a short training period, he had been transferred to Wichita, where as a junior executive, he helped establish routes to Tulsa, Dodge City, Abilene, and Omaha. Then had come the offer from the young and growing Great Plains Overland Stage Company. It had been one he could not refuse. For the past six years, he had worked out of the Great Plains home office in Denver, planning and setting up routes north, south, and west of the booming Mile High City.

A prairie dog scurried across the path and dived into a hole. Dayton thought of the women he had met over the years. Some had tried to press him into marriage, but he would have none of it. Like he always said, marrying the wrong woman would be worse than not marrying at all.

From deep within him, a barbed accusation seemed to stab at his brain. *Maybe you are just too cautious, Chance Dayton. So Lily threw you over for a fat rich man. All women are not like her. If you are ever going to settle down and get married, you may have to take a woman who does not ring the bell you keep expecting to hear.*

The ruggedly handsome man shook his head again, as if he could rid himself of the thought the way a dog shakes off water. Up ahead, his eye caught a movement.

Pulling his horse to a halt, he squinted against the glare. Among the cottonwoods on the river's bank some five hundred yards ahead, several men were milling about. Dayton blinked and squinted again. *Good heavens,* he thought. *They can't do that.* . . . At that moment he saw a rope sail over a cottonwood limb. The end of the rope was in the form of a hangman's noose.

He touched the horse's sides with his spurs, and the startled animal lunged forward, throwing snow and sod into the air. Dayton forced it into a full gallop.

As the thundering horse carried him nearer, Dayton saw a form lifted upward by two men and placed on a saddled horse. Another man suddenly pointed in Dayton's direction. As the faces turned toward him, he bellowed, *"Hold it!"*

One of the men dropped the noose over the victim's head and drew it up tight as Dayton reined his mount to a halt. Without drawing his gun, he growled, "What's going on here?"

There were three men in the lynching party. Two of them were young and, by their resemblance, seemed to be of the same family. A quick glance at the older man convinced Dayton that he was their father.

Sitting on a white-stockinged bay gelding was a young man no more than twenty years old. He had shaggy blond hair and was somewhat stocky in build. The noose tugged precariously at his neck. His hands were tied behind him, and his face was blanched in terror, a purple ring of fear encircling his mouth.

"Some old-fashioned justice," came the older man's raspy reply to Dayton's question. "And whoever you are, there's nothing you can do about it."

"You're the law, are you?" challenged Dayton.

"All that's necessary," clipped the man, jutting his jaw.

Unbuttoning his sheepskin coat, Dayton asked, "What's the charge against this man?"

"It's none of your affair, mister!" came the stern

64

reply. "Now you just ride on, and you'll get to where you were headed."

Pulling out an official-looking document and holding it out for the older man to see, Dayton said, "I am acting for the law. I am empowered by the Great Plains Overland Stage Company to bring to justice the killer of one of our guards. The killer's name is Dakota Smith. Now . . . I asked you a question. What is the charge against this man?"

The older man's deeply lined face pinched. "Where you from, mister?"

"I rode here from Fort Keogh."

"That's Logan Banner's town, Pa!" spoke up one of the sons.

"That right?" queried the older man, squinting and cocking his head sideways. "You come from Banner's town?"

"The same," Dayton answered, still sitting his horse, hoping the older man would believe that he had the authority to interfere.

"Pa, don't mix with him!" warned the same son. "I've heard tell Banner will—"

"Shut up, Harvey!" snapped the older man.

"Please, mister!" cried the intended victim from his hazardous position on the back of the horse. "Don't let them hang me. I'm innocent! I didn't kill his son! I'm not Dakota Smith. I'm—"

"You shut up, Dakota!" railed the old man. "You killed Paul, and we both know it."

"Just a minute!" Dayton bellowed, eyeing the old man. "Who are *you*?"

"I'm Ben Warren," the man said sourly. Pointing a crooked finger toward his sons, he added, "And these are my boys, Clarence and Harvey." Pointing the same finger at the trembling young man with the rope on his neck, he said, "And that dirty skunk is Dakota Smith. If he says he ain't, he's lyin'! He gunned down my youngest, Paul. Murdered him in cold blood!"

Dayton knew that the young man on the horse was not Dakota Smith. He came nowhere near fitting the description. The only possible similarity was that both he and Dakota Smith had yellow-blond hair. Dayton was going to have to convince Ben Warren and his sons of this fact without stirring any emotions. Any sudden outburst could spook the horse. And if it bolted, the innocent young man would die.

"Now, Mr. Warren," Dayton said in a quiet, level tone, "the man you have here is not the outlaw you're looking for. I know Dakota Smith was in Baker, and I know he killed a young rancher. But—"

"He sure did!" cut in the old man. "Goaded Paul into a gunfight, knowin' he wasn't no gunfighter. Paul's gun wasn't slung low or even tied down. His hands were just like mine, rough and callused from hard work. It was murder, mister. Cold-blooded murder!"

Holding his voice calm, Dayton said, "This man is not Dakota Smith, Mr. Warren. I will be glad to explain how I know that, but first I want the rope taken off the man's neck."

Harvey Warren started toward the bay gelding, but his father snapped a command that was like the slash of a whip. "Harvey! You stay put!"

"But, Pa," argued Harvey, "the man said—"

"I don't care what he said!" The old man's eyes flashed fire. "Harvey, who told you to put that noose on his neck?"

The youthful Warren swallowed hard and said, "You did, Pa."

Regarding Harvey with a hard glare, Ben said, "Then don't you take it off till I tell you! Understand?"

"Yes, Pa," said Harvey, dipping his chin.

"Look, Mr. Warren," Dayton said through his clenched teeth, "I want that man cut loose. I mean *now!*"

"You ain't got no jurisdiction here, mister," retorted Warren. "Now ride on like I told you. We're gonna have us some justice here, and you ain't gettin' in the way."

Dayton was tempted to pull his gun, but he feared that one of the Warrens might be fool enough to retaliate. Any gunfire would hang the young man on the horse.

Ben Warren continued. "This dirty snake killed my son Paul yesterday morning. Me and the boys got a description of him and his horse and took out after him. We run up on him no more than twenty minutes ago. Now it's *his* turn to die."

"Pa," spoke up Clarence, the older of the two sons, "why don't you quit jawin' and get on with the hangin'?"

Pointing a stiff finger at his son, Warren said, "You shut your trap, hear me? We'll hang him when I say. 'Sides, it's good for him to sit there and think on what he done."

"I tell you," Dayton said, "you've got the wrong man. Dakota Smith is blond, but that's where this man's resemblance to him stops. Dakota Smith is quite slender. This man would outweigh him by thirty pounds."

"Says you!" snarled Warren.

"Not only that," said Dayton, ignoring the retort, "but Dakota Smith wears two guns. This man was wearing only one."

While the old man was digesting that statement, Dayton swung his gaze to the victim, and said, "What is your name, son?"

"Dean Wellman, sir," came the nervous reply. "I'm from Bismarck. I . . . I wasn't even in Baker. I was visiting some relatives who have a farm a few miles this side of Baker. I was riding for home when these men rode up and drew their guns on me."

"He's lyin'!" Ben Warren growled. "He's Dakota Smith. He killed my boy!"

"Did he try to run away when you rode up on him?" asked the ex-cavalry officer, pinning Ben Warren with his glare.

"Well, no," came the man's reply.

"Don't you think if he was your son's killer, he would have tried to get away?"

"Nope. He hung around Baker all morning after he killed Paul. Seems like he was just defyin' us to come after him."

Wellman's horse bobbed its head and snorted, shifting its hindquarters. "Whoa, boy!" Wellman gasped.

Dayton pulled his lips tight against his teeth. "The least you can do is check out this lad's story, Mr. Warren. Let him take you to his relatives' farm."

Ben Warren's face soured. "So Dakota Smith has some relatives near Baker—they'd just lie for him! That's probably why we caught up to him this soon. He no doubt had stopped to see them." Pointing at the horse, he added, "Witnesses said Dakota was ridin' a bay with four white stockin's. Had a blaze face."

With a dark flush mounting to his cheeks, Dayton countered, "You can't hang a man for the horse he rides. You know as well as I do that there are lots of bays with those same markings. Now, I want Dean Wellman free of that rope. You release him, take your rope and your boys, and go on home. Do what I tell you, and I'll forget this incident."

Ben Warren bristled. "Nobody kills a Warren and rides away scot-free, mister. *Nobody!*"

"Look, Warren!" rumbled Dayton. "You hang this man, and you'll hang yourself! So will your sons!"

Clarence Warren, who stood near his father, shouted angrily, "We're only carryin' out justice for Paul, mister. There ain't no law in Baker—no sheriff and no marshal. So it's every dog for himself. This mangy cur murdered my brother, and he's gonna die!"

"I did not murder your brother," gasped Dean Wellman, straining against the rope that was chafing his skin. "I tell you, I'm not Dakota Smith!" Fear convulsed his young features, turning his complexion livid. His horse was becoming jumpy.

Dayton was desperate. "Don't you realize what you're doing?" he questioned. "You are about to do to someone else's son what Dakota Smith did to yours."

"He *is* Dakota Smith!" Warren bellowed. "He murdered my son, and he's gonna pay!" In blind fury, the old man dashed toward Wellman and slapped the horse's rump savagely.

Wellman screamed wildly when the horse bolted. Ben Warren whipped out his gun, but not before Dayton drew and fired. As Warren went down, his sons began shooting at the ex-cavalry officer, but Dayton fired back. Guns were roaring. Dayton was about to fire again, when he felt his horse buckle under him. Suddenly he felt a blow like a sledgehammer hit his skull. He seemed to be falling faster than the animal beneath him. A deep, dark vortex sucked him out of the world.

The sun was nearly touching the western horizon when Dayton became aware that he was back in the world. He could feel the cold, hard ground against his back. There was no sound except for his own labored breathing. His head throbbed as he tried to open his eyes. The left one fluttered, letting in painful shafts of light. Quickly, he closed it again.

Clenching his teeth against the pain in his head, Dayton tried to move his body. Something was wrong . . . both legs were paralyzed! They would not move.

Wait a minute . . . the right leg. It did move. Yes! The right leg seemed to be elevated. He was lying in an awkward position, and his left leg was numb. No feeling at all. It was as if it had been amputated. Fear flooded his mind. Where was he? What had happened?

His left eye popped open, but the brilliant light forced it shut again. His head was spinning. The hard earth beneath him seemed to whirl.

Totally disoriented, he willed the spinning sensation to stop. Slowly, he opened and closed the left eye, allowing it to adjust to the light. What was wrong with his right eye? Had it gone blind?

As the vision cleared in the left eye, Dayton focused

on the red and orange that enflamed the scattered clouds above him. Slowly, he lifted his head. When he saw the dark, lifeless form of his dead horse against the setting sun, it all came back. The Warrens . . . the gunfire . . . and Dean Wellman!

Suddenly, Dayton realized he was not alone. Beyond his horse was another figure, this one of a man. His first reaction was to go for his gun, but when he moved his arm, a pain like a hot iron ran across his forehead.

Then the figure moved. Dayton knew that he was at the mercy of the man and hoped that it wasn't one of the Warrens, returned to finish the job of killing him.

"Let me help you get out from under the horse," the man said as he approached Dayton, squatting to where he lay.

With that, Dayton realized why his left leg was numb. The horse was lying on it. He remembered the animal caving in underneath him when the shooting started.

"I'd appreciate it," he said.

Straining and pulling against the numb leg while the other man lifted the dead animal, Dayton finally worked himself free. Immediately the leg began to tingle, as though a thousand needles were puncturing the skin.

He waited until the tingling had subsided before attempting to stand up. Gaining his feet, he limped about for several moments. Slowly the feeling was returning to his leg, and he grew confident that it was not broken.

"So you're Dayton," the tall, gray-haired man said. "I was hoping we'd run into each other. "I'm Logan Banner, marshal of Fort Keogh."

Dayton took the other man's outstretched hand. "Pleased to meet you, Marshal. Your name carries a lot of weight in these parts, I've found. Not enough, though, to have prevented that," he said, pointing to the tree from which the lifeless body of Dean Wellman hung. The young man's face was bloated and purple. The corpse twisted slightly in the breeze, causing the taut rope to give off a popping, staccato sound as it rubbed against the limb overhead.

Unconsciously, Dayton's hand went to his head. He winced when the fingers touched the spot on his temple where the bullet had grazed him. The bleeding had stopped.

Cautiously exploring further with his fingertips, he solved the mystery of the right eye. It was caked shut with blood. The angle at which his head had lain while he was unconscious had allowed the blood to trickle into his eye.

Within moments he had worked the dried blood loose enough for the eye to open.

"Looks as though you took quite a beating," Banner remarked. "You mind telling me who's behind all this?"

Dayton began the story, recalling that a bullet he had fired had downed Ben Warren. His gaze swept over the prairie as he continued. There was nothing moving anywhere, not on either side of the river. Clarence and Harvey Warren must have gathered up the body of their father and headed for home.

The older man looked grim when Dayton finished his story. Banner told Dayton that he would go after the two Warren brothers—they were accessories to Dean Wellman's murder—but first things first. Dakota Smith had gunned down Jim Chapman in cold blood, and he was at the top of the list.

Dayton and the rawboned lawman climbed the tree in the vague light of the dying day and cut down Dean Wellman's body. Limping slightly, Dayton roamed the flat land with Banner, gathering rocks for the young man's burial ground. It was totally dark by the time Wellman was completely covered by the mound of stone.

Stripping the saddle and bedroll from his dead horse, Dayton found a satisfactory spot among the cottonwoods to spend the night. He and the marshal rolled out their beds on the ground. Gathering some sticks, they built a fire and ate a meal from the provisions in their saddlebags.

After feeding the fire, Dayton slipped into his bedroll and lay in the darkness under the star-bedecked sky. Studying the shimmering heavens, he thought about the events of the last few days. He wondered why life sometimes was so unfair. So many people had lost their lives just for being in the wrong place at the wrong time.

And then he thought of Polly Temple, and the way she had comforted Martha Dugan. When he thought of Polly, a warm, tingling sensation ran through him, and soon he found himself relaxing into sleep.

As Dayton drifted off to sleep a few yards away, Marshal Logan Banner lay awake with his own thoughts. He pictured his son, Lindsey, and then Jim Chapman, the man who had become a son to him in his heart. Why did everyone he loved have to be taken away from him? Why did Jim have to die so young? And then he thought of Dakota Smith. While Jim lay cold in his grave, that killer was warm, breathing, and enjoying the pleasures of life. It was also Dakota Smith's fault that young Dean Wellman would never see another sunrise.

A coldness came over the marshal that was deeper than the frostbitten night. *I'll get you, Dakota Smith*, Banner thought. *I'll get you if it's the last thing I ever do.* With fresh hatred for the killer burning within, he fell into a deep sleep.

Chapter Five

The next morning, Marshal Logan Banner and Chance Dayton parted company. Dayton had to return to his job—the inaugural run of the Great Plains stage to Fargo had been delayed long enough—and Banner was determined to find his deputy's killer. The marshal told the ex-cavalry officer that he was not likely to see him again until Dakota Smith was in his custody—or in his grave.

Dayton spent the day on the trail, made camp that night, and then continued on into the town of Fort Keogh the next morning. When he rode into town just before noon and walked into the stage office, he was greeted by William Thomas and Fred Meade. Dayton told them what had happened during his search for Dakota Smith and how Banner had helped him.

After expressing his concern for the marshal's well-being, Thomas said, "Jenkins and Hillyer are here. They and the passengers are staying at the hotel."

Turning to Meade, Dayton said, "May I see the passenger list?"

As the agent laid it in his hand, Dayton saw quickly that there would be six passengers besides himself on the journey. Only one of them was not going all the way to Fargo.

Reading aloud, Dayton scanned the list. "Miss Barbara Stevens—Fargo. Mr. and Mrs. Carl Weinberger—Fargo. Miss Melody R—"

Both men studied Dayton. "Someone you know?" Meade asked.

"Yeah," nodded the handsome man. "Melody Rogers. She's a dance-hall queen out of Denver. Songbird. She's the main attraction at Denver's biggest saloon."

Dayton did not volunteer the fact that he and Melody had at one time become close. She had even tried to rope him into marriage. Melody was beautiful and a lot of fun, but marriage material she was not. He wondered why she was going to Fargo.

"Mrs. Polly Temple—Bismarck," Dayton continued, and for a moment his voice faltered as he realized that the captivating woman he had met the other day was married. "Cecil Knowlton—Fargo," he forced himself to go on. "I see he's booked to take the train on to Minneapolis."

Meade offered Dayton the use of his room upstairs to freshen up. Dayton retrieved his travel bag from the back room of the stage office and headed upstairs. After a hot bath, he shaved and put on fresh clothes. Then he headed back down to the office, where Fred Meade and William Thomas were waiting with two other men.

"Chance Dayton," Thomas said. "Come shake hands with F.E. Jenkins and Wayne Hillyer."

Dayton was impressed by the solid grip of F.E. Jenkins. The veteran stagecoach driver was short and quite stoutly built. Dayton figured him to be somewhere around fifty. There was silver in his temples, and his face was weatherworn. He wore bib overalls, a heavy mackinaw, and a tattered, sweat-stained hat. There was an obvious lump on one side of his jaw—tobacco, Dayton figured, which explained why he had been sitting beside a brass spittoon.

F.E.'s reputation had preceded him. Dayton had been told that he was strong as a bull and known to be handy in a fistfight. "He's tough as an old boot," someone had said, "and swears a blue streak." More than anything else, F.E. Jenkins was known for his expertise with a team of horses. The big animals readily responded to his voice and his touch on the reins.

Dayton judged a man by the way he shook hands, and Wayne Hillyer had as hale and masculine a grip as his partner. Just under six feet in height and of medium build, Hillyer was friendly and clean-cut, and would be thirty-five on his next birthday. He was known to have nerves of steel and to be expert with shotgun, rifle, and revolver.

After a few minutes discussing the upcoming trip, the five men walked to the hotel dining room for lunch. During the meal, they talked of weather, relay stations, and Indians. Thomas pointed out the importance of this first run. Its success would open the way toward a profitable venture for the company, enabling it to branch out with other runs.

While Thomas was talking, Dayton saw that Hillyer had his eyes focused on something behind him. Hillyer smiled and said, "Mmm-mmm! Turn around, Chance, and feast your peepers on that!"

Dayton turned and looked over his shoulder to see Melody Rogers headed his way. A smile parted her lips as their eyes met.

Melody was in her late twenties. She had flaming red hair, done in an upsweep, and was quite pretty, even without her heavy makeup. Her eyes were deep blue, her height five feet seven inches, and she weighed a hundred and twenty-five pounds. She was a well-proportioned woman, and she knew it.

Dayton was on his feet when she reached the table. "Chance, darling!" she exclaimed. "It *is* you!" With that, she wrapped her arms around him as the other men at the table stood up. She planted a warm, lingering kiss on his lips.

Finding himself a bit nonplussed, the Great Plains agent in charge of establishing new routes cleared his throat, and said, "Gentlemen, may I present Miss Melody Rogers."

Still clinging to Dayton's muscular arm, the vivacious woman smiled and said, "Good afternoon, gentlemen."

Hillyer displayed a broad grin and gasped, "Hey, Chance, you got any more friends like this?"

Melody giggled. Reaching across the table with an extended forefinger, she touched the tip of the shotgunner's nose and said, "You're cute!"

Hillyer crimsoned.

Dayton introduced each man to Melody, then asked her to sit down. "Oh, no," she said, squeezing his hand. "I must be getting along. I couldn't pass by without speaking to you, though. Are you here for the ceremony tomorrow? They said our delay was—why, Chance, darling! They said the trip was being postponed because a big man in the company who was to ride the stagecoach all the way to Fargo had been called away. Darling, it's *you*, isn't it?"

"Yes." Dayton nodded, wishing she would back off and let him breathe. "I saw your name on the passenger list."

"And you didn't look me up? Why, Chance Dayton, what is this world coming to? I'm beginning to wonder about our relationship!"

"I wasn't aware we had one," Dayton said flatly. "Anyhow, I've only been back a couple of hours. I was wondering, though, why you're going to Fargo."

"It's my new job, honey," she said, flashing her big smile. "I'm going to work in Fargo at the Silver Horse! You *will* come and hear me sing, won't you?"

Dayton hesitated.

"I don't know about him," Hillyer cut in, "but I will sure be there, Miss Melody!"

76

The flamboyant woman giggled again. "You *are* a cutie-pie!" Turning back to Dayton, she said, "Oh, darling, I am so glad we'll be riding together on the trip." Pecking his cheek, she excused herself and flitted away, swinging her hips.

Hillyer was totally taken by the saloon singer. He watched her until she passed out of sight. Bringing his gaze to Dayton, who was wiping lipstick from his face with a napkin, he asked, "Just what is your relationship with her, Chance?"

"There is none," Dayton said levelly. "We're just friends."

At that moment, a middle-aged man with bloodshot eyes and a red bulbous nose approached the table. Reeking of whiskey, he said, "Good afternoon, gentlemen. My name is Cecil Knowlton. I'll be riding the stagecoach to Fargo."

"We hope you will enjoy the trip, Mr. Knowlton," Dayton said. "Didn't I see in our records that you're taking the train from Fargo to Minneapolis?"

"Yes, that is true. I am a drummer for the Apex Tool Company in Minneapolis. I'm glad you people are starting the stagecoach route. It's going to help my business. Make it much easier for me to get about in Montana and Dakota."

"We hope many others will feel just as you do, Mr. Knowlton," Thomas spoke up.

Morning came to Fort Keogh, bright and clear. The air was cold and crisp, with a raw wind blowing in from the north.

The bright red Concord stagecoach stood in the middle of the street, reflecting the sunlight. Four horses fiddled against their harness, stamping and blowing. They were eager to run. Breath came from their nostrils, appearing momentarily in vaporous plumes, then dissipating skyward.

The luggage was aboard and tied down. A single red ribbon surrounded the entire rig, attached to the tops of waist-high stakes that had been driven into the street. A small brass band was playing music in front of the stage office, and citizens of the town were gathering.

Jenkins and Hillyer stood near the office door beside Dayton and Thomas. Fred Meade was on the boardwalk clearing a path for the passengers, who were arriving from the hotel. In the lead was Cecil Knowlton, who was greeting everyone with a hearty "Good morning!"

Dayton hoped the man's obvious passion for whiskey would not be a problem on the trip. Abruptly his attention was drawn to Polly Temple, who was standing in front of the stage office with another young woman. The two were being greeted by Fred Meade. Running the passenger list through his mind, he knew this had to be Miss Barbara Stevens.

Dayton's first impression was that she was quite plain. She was a bit thin and had straight, mouse-brown hair, and her close-fitting coat said little for her figure.

But when Polly Temple appeared after Barbara, she nearly stopped Dayton's heart. Each time he saw her, her stunning beauty captured him all over again. He had never seen a face so perfect . . . so indescribably beautiful. Never had he seen eyes so filled with expression and personality. Her walk was smooth and feminine, her head held erect. This was a genuine *lady*. But a married lady.

Wearing a wide grin, Fred Meade guided the young women toward the two Great Plains executives. "Gentlemen," he said, "may I present Miss Barbara Stevens. I believe you have met Mrs. Temple before."

The cold air that surrounded the crowd that morning was nothing compared to the arctic chill that came over Dayton when he heard Polly Temple addressed by her married title. All his life he had waited to meet a woman like her, and she was pledged to love someone

else. How could this happen to him? Wasn't the heart-
ache he had suffered over Lily Andrews enough for one
man's lifetime?

Suddenly he was aware that Polly was addressing
him. ". . . Fort Abraham Lincoln?"

His brain felt numb. "Excuse me, ma'am?"

Smiling pleasantly, Polly repeated her question. "Mr.
Meade tells me you set up the route to Fargo. When
you've been in Bismarck, have you ever visited Fort
Abraham Lincoln?"

"Yes, ma'am, I have," Dayton replied.

Polly started to ask another question, when Meade
ushered up an elderly couple, whom he introduced as
Mr. and Mrs. Carl Weinberger. The old man was evi-
dently in poor health. His face was pale and drawn, and
he walked with shoulders drooped.

Dayton greeted the Weinbergers and then swung his
line of sight back to Polly. Along with Barbara Stevens,
her attention was on the band.

While Dayton battled his runaway heart—and the
cold disappointment of knowing that Polly was married—
Melody Rogers put in her appearance. He knew she
had planned it that way. She always had to have a grand
entrance.

Swinging her hips as only she could do, the dance-
hall queen floated up the boardwalk. Like a magnet,
she drew the eyes of the men in the crowd. As she
came near Dayton, he could tell she was loaded with
perfume and had thickened her makeup. Her hair re-
sembled flame in the brilliant sunshine.

Melody joined the circle of passengers, greeting each
one. She also addressed Jenkins, William Thomas, and
Wayne Hillyer—again making the shotgunner redden
by calling him cutie-pie. Sliding a gloved hand inside
Dayton's arm, she breathed warmly, "Good morning,
Chance darling."

The handsome man gave her a tight smile.

Thomas signaled for the band to wind it up, and

when the last notes had died out in the air, he stepped forth and addressed the crowd. He opened with a short speech, telling of the company's interest in the growth and prosperity of their town and the expansion of the West.

Next Thomas introduced the driver and shotgunner, then presented Dayton, describing his vital role in setting up the new route. He then ceremoniously cut the red ribbon that surrounded the stagecoach.

While the band resumed playing, the passengers boarded the stagecoach and took their places beneath heavy buffalo robes. Hillyer closed the door and followed the stout-bodied driver up to the box.

Jenkins cracked his whip, and the bright-red Concord rolled out of town as the band played "The Girl I Left Behind Me."

From the driver's seat, Jenkins spit a brown stream over the side of the stagecoach and swore at the frigid air.

"What's the matter, old boy?" queried Hillyer, the shotgun guard, with a sly grin. "Wishing you were back in California?"

Wiping tobacco juice from one corner of his mouth with the back of a gloved hand, the stout-bodied Jenkins said, "At least in California I didn't have to worry about freezin'. This flat, frozen, monotonous iceberg leaves somethin' to be desired, I'll tell you."

"I bet it'll look better when you get the first week's pay," Hillyer commented.

Jenkins cocked his head. "Well, now, you might have somethin' there. I'll admit the pay with this outfit is the best I've ever had."

The tough old driver swore at one of the horses for being lazy.

Hillyer slitted his eyes against the glare of the snow and examined the broad sweep of the prairie. He hoped the Sioux would not do damage to the stage line the way they had done to the railroad.

Inside the stagecoach, Dayton sat on the uncomfortable middle seat, facing forward. On the front seat, riding backward, were Polly Temple, Barbara Stevens, and Melody Rogers. On the rear seat, Maude Weinberger sat between her husband, Carl, who suffered periodic coughing spells, and Cecil Knowlton. The elderly woman eyed Knowlton with disgust each time he pulled the small flask from his coat and took a nip.

Dayton rocked on the middle seat to the rhythm of the swaying coach, pulling the buffalo robe close around him. It was a constant effort to keep his eyes off Polly. She was absolutely the most fascinating female he had ever seen. He silently hoped that her husband realized and appreciated the prize that he had.

Melody tugged at the furry robe that covered her body and tucked it tight under her chin. She smiled warmly at the handsome Great Plains agent and said, "I've missed you, Chance darling."

Dayton smiled tightly and made no comment.

"Do you plan to be in Fargo often?" Melody asked.

"No," he replied, keeping Polly in focus from the corner of his eye. "Once a new route is established, I head back to Denver to begin paperwork on another one."

"Well, then, I don't know whether I want to move to Fargo or not," she said in a plaintive tone. "How will I go on without you? I mean, we have meant so much to each other."

It was evident to the other passengers that the heavily painted dance-hall queen was trying to impress upon them that she and the good-looking Dayton had once been very close.

Her dark red lips in a pout, Melody said, "We just can't be apart too long, darling. You must find time to come to Fargo."

Chuckling to make light of Melody's talk, Dayton

said, "You've managed quite well without me nearby, Melody. Besides the way men flock to you, there'll be no time for you to get lonesome."

"But I would rather be with you," she cooed.

Dayton's discomfort under Melody's pressure was quite obvious. Barbara Stevens came to his rescue by turning to the painted lady and saying, "Melody, didn't you have a good job in Denver?"

"Oh, yes," answered the redhead.

"Why did you leave it to go to Fargo?"

One thing that Melody liked to do was talk about herself, and she eagerly told of her success at Denver's largest and most popular saloon. Over the years, she had been presented with many offers by saloon and dance-hall operators from Kansas City to San Francisco, but her boss in Denver had found her so valuable that he had always given her raises attractive enough to keep her.

However, in late September, Langford Best, the owner of Fargo's famous Silver Horse Saloon, had come to Denver to make her a superlative offer. Not only would she receive more than double in salary, but she would also become a partner. Her financial future would be rock solid. When she became too old to sing and attract the crowds, she would still have a reliable income.

Maude Weinberger interrupted. "Miss Rogers, don't you have a higher goal in life than to hang around smoke-filled saloons and dance halls? What about a husband and children? And a home?"

Taken aback by the older woman's brash questioning, Melody looked at her blankly for a few minutes and then replied, "I've had my proposals of marriage, Mrs. Weinberger. But never from the right man. And even if I do get a proposal from him, I don't want children. Having children destroys a woman's figure."

"It's a good thing your mother wasn't worried about hers, wouldn't you say?" Maude's eyes were petulant.

Melody's features stiffened with anger. "My mother

didn't want me, ma'am," she said icily. "I was never meant to be. She was a soiled dove in a Wichita brothel and had no idea who my father was. She gave me away when I was four years old."

The older woman's face pinched with pity. "I . . . I'm sorry, honey," she said apologetically. "Please forgive this old woman for sticking her nose in."

"Forget it," clipped Melody, running her suggestive gaze back to Dayton's face. His eyes were on Polly.

Melody started to speak, desiring his attention for herself, when Jenkins's voice cut the air. "Way station comin' up!"

Crew and passengers warmed themselves inside the station and drank coffee while the stationmaster hooked up a fresh team to the big red Concord. Within half an hour they were in motion again.

When Carl Weinberger went into a coughing spasm, Cecil Knowlton pulled out his flask and, reaching across Maude, offered it to the ailing man. "Little swig of this will help that cough, Mr. Weinberger. Just go ahead and—"

"He has medicine, sir!" Maude rasped. "My husband doesn't drink."

Huddling low in his buffalo robe, the elderly man hacked and said, "Appreciate it, Mr. Knowlton, but I'll be all right."

Knowlton uncapped the slender vessel, took a healthy gulp, and ceremoniously recapped it. He burped and said, "Hey, everybody! We've got a long haul ahead of us. Let's get better acquainted. It'll take our minds off the cold. We've heard all about Miss Rogers, here, so I'll be next." Leaning forward, he looked at Melody with a twinkle in his bloodshot eyes and said, "Honey, if I were ten years younger, I would try to romance you myself."

"Thank God for little favors," said the painted woman dryly.

Ignoring the insult, Knowlton proceeded. "You all know my name. Cecil V. Knowlton. The V stands for Vance. That was my grandfather's name, on my mother's side, that is."

Polly looked at Dayton as Knowlton's voice droned on. She smiled, raised her eyes toward the roof of the coach, and shook her head. Dayton smiled back and nodded in agreement. Cecil V. Knowlton was a bore.

The drummer went on, giving every uninteresting detail of his job for the Apex Tool Company of Minneapolis. He was on his way there to pick up some samples, he explained, adding that the new stage route was certainly going to make his job easier.

When he stopped to take a drink from his flask, Maude Weinberger quickly spoke up and said, "Well, we've heard all about our tool drummer, so let me explain about Carl and myself."

Knowlton sat in sudden silence as the woman took over, her frail husband huddled next to her, hacking and wheezing. Maude explained that she and Carl were nearing seventy years of age, and his sickness had taken its toll on their finances. Carl had been unable to work for the past three years. His older brother had recently died and left him a house in Fargo. They were going there to live out the rest of their days.

Melody looked sympathetically at the elderly couple, flat broke and, but for a meager stroke of luck, homeless in their sunset years. She was confident about her decision to move to Fargo; there would be no poverty for her when she got old.

Later, after a hearty lunch at the next way station, a fresh team pulled the Concord onward. As the vehicle rocked and the wheels settled into their customary drone, Cecil Knowlton took another swig from his freshly filled flask and said, "Well, we still haven't heard from Miss Stevens, Mrs. Temple, or from you, Mr. Dayton."

Dayton eyed the man casually and said, "Everybody knows why I'm aboard."

"But we don't know much about you," Knowlton parried. "I've got a feeling Miss Rogers could tell us some interesting things."

Melody smiled as if to say that the red-nosed man was right.

"I doubt that what Miss Rogers has to say would interest anyone," Dayton answered levelly. "There's not much to tell. I'm originally from Columbus, Ohio. I fought in the Civil War as a captain in the Union cavalry, and I've been in the transportation business since the summer of sixty-five."

"Never been married?" asked Knowlton.

"No."

"Sounds to me like Miss Rogers would like to alter that."

Dayton grinned and shook his head. "If I ever do get married, sir, I will want children."

Melody eyed him coyly and said, "For you I might change my mind."

Dayton said nothing, fearing that any response he made might come out wrong. Knowlton saw that Dayton's story was finished, so he spoke to the two young women who sat side by side. "What about you two?"

Barbara and Polly glanced at each other. Neither one cared to comment on herself, but since the others had done so, there was no escaping it.

Reluctantly, Barbara went first. "I am from Cheyenne," she said, looking toward the floor. "I . . . I am on my way to Fargo to . . . to get married."

"Why, that's wonderful, honey," Maude said. "Tell us about your young man."

Barbara lifted a hand from beneath the heavy robe to brush the straight brown hair from her well-scrubbed face. Lifting her eyes to meet Maude's inquisitive gaze, she replied, "His name is John Swenson."

"And he lives in Fargo?"

"Outside of Fargo, ma'am. He's a farmer. His place is almost seventeen or eighteen miles east of town."

"What does he raise on his farm?" The question came from Dayton. The young woman was obviously quite nervous, and some relatively impersonal questions, he reasoned, might ease her tension.

Knowlton was pouring whiskey down his throat as though it were water. Maude wanted to snatch the flask from his hand and throw it out the loosely covered window.

In reply to Dayton, Barbara smiled shyly, saying, "John raises mainly potatoes and sugar beets. Next spring he is planning also to plant carrots. With the railhead at Fargo, he has an unlimited market."

"How many acres does he farm?" Dayton queried.

Polly, who had become acquainted with Barbara in Fort Keogh's hotel, knew why the reserved woman was nervous. She appreciated Dayton's kindness and smiled at him to tell him so.

Polly's warm smile almost made him forget his question, until Barbara answered, "He has four hundred acres."

"That ought to keep him busy," Dayton commented.

"Along with four milk cows, a dozen hogs, four draft horses, and a yard full of chickens." Barbara smiled, feeling more at ease.

Knowlton drained his flask and capped it. He shocked Maude Weinberger by stuffing it into a coat pocket and producing another one. She was glad the air was cold. It helped stifle the strong odor of alcohol on his breath.

Dayton noticed Knowlton switch flasks. Leaning close to the liquid-eyed man, he said, "Mr. Knowlton, I think you've had enough."

Knowlton eyed him sluggishly and said, "I know how much ish enough, kid. An' I ain't had it yet."

Reaching for the flask, Dayton said, "Let me hold that for you. These people have paid their fare the same as you. Riding with a drunk man is not very pleasant."

Swinging the flask over his head to pull it out of Dayton's reach, Knowlton belched and said, "I ain't drunk, Dayton. Now, a man hash a right to ship a little whiskey on a trip."

Holding out an open hand, the Great Plains agent said harshly, "You can either give it to me, or I'm going to take it. Choice is yours."

Bleary-eyed, the tool drummer focused clearly on Dayton's face long enough to see that he meant business. He lowered the flask, and as Dayton pulled it from his fingers, Knowlton belched again and mumbled something that no one understood.

Returning to the subject at hand, Dayton swung back to face Barbara. "Sounds like your John Swenson is an industrious man."

"His parents were successful farmers in Sweden," she remarked, smiling. "John will do as well as his father, I'm sure."

"It will probably mean a lot of work for you," Maude spoke up.

"I won't mind, ma'am," Barbara said pleasantly. "I was raised on a farm. I know what hard work is."

Melody's curiosity had been aroused. Twisting in the seat to look at Barbara, she asked, "How did you two ever meet?"

Barbara's face flushed, and she dropped her gaze to the floor.

"Hey, I'm sorry, kid," Melody said. "Didn't mean to hit a nerve."

Looking up into Melody's painted face, Barbara said, "It's going to sound a bit strange, but John and I have never met."

"Never met?" gasped the dance-hall singer with amazement. "You are going to marry a man you never met? It's strange, all right. How in this world—"

"She's a mail-order bride," Polly cut in, throwing Melody a warning look. "And I think it's wonderful."

"Oh, how romantic!" exclaimed Maude.

Melody thought the idea was disgusting, but kept that sentiment to herself. Her only comment was, "Well, it's different. I'll say that much."

"How did you make contact with him?" asked Maude.

Over Carl's coughing spasm, Barbara explained that John Swenson had placed an advertisement in the *Cheyenne Gazette*. He was looking for a wife, it said, who was in good physical health, between twenty and thirty years of age, and had farming experience. Barbara had answered the advertisement, and a letter-writing relationship had developed.

Still somewhat disconcerted, Melody asked, "What does your mail-order groom look like?"

"He's . . . he's six feet tall," replied the plain-faced young woman. "He weighs a hundred and ninety pounds, and he has blue eyes and blond hair."

"What I mean," said Melody, "is what does he *look* like? Is he handsome?"

"I don't know," came the quiet answer. "We agreed in correspondence that our relationship would not be founded on physical attraction, but on character and inward qualities. We have never exchanged photographs."

Melody closed her eyes and shook her head. Such behavior in her way of thinking was absolutely insane.

"But I am somewhat apprehensive," Barbara admitted. "I have this gnawing fear that John is expecting me to be pretty."

"Beauty is as beauty does," Maude said with a tone of encouragement. "I have an idea your John is going to think you are the prettiest woman in the world."

"Oh, I hope so, Mrs. Weinberger," Barbara said. "But I sure do wish I looked like Polly. She really *is* the prettiest woman in the world!"

Polly's face tinted. Melody told herself that was only Barbara's opinion. But as her eyes settled on Dayton's face, she would have taken bets that it was his opinion, too.

As Jenkins's whip popped outside, followed by a string of foul words, the lot fell on Polly to tell her story.

"Guess I'm last," she said with a smile. "I am on my way to Fort Abraham Lincoln to visit my father, so I will be getting off at Bismarck. I plan to stay with him until the next time this stage heads east through Bismarck. I will then go on to visit my cousin Louise Stedham and her husband in Fargo. Greg is in the hardware business there."

Knowlton, who had sat sullen and quiet in his corner since losing his liquor, spruced up at the sound of a familiar name. "I know him," he slurred. "Greg Stedham carriesh my toolsh in hish shtore!"

Polly nodded polite acknowledgment to the inebriated tool drummer.

Assuming Polly's father to be a military man, Dayton was about to ask his rank when Maude asked, "Polly, what does your husband do for a living?"

The attractive blond woman lowered her eyes briefly and then raised them slowly to meet the older woman's gaze. Unaware of Dayton's fascination for her, Polly replied, "My husband is dead, Mrs. Weinberger."

Dayton was totally stunned. Had he heard correctly? He so desperately wanted her to be single . . . possibly his ears had made him hear what he *wanted* to hear.

But now, Polly's explanation was filtering through.

"My husband was Sergeant Will Temple. He was based at Fort Laramie. Will was killed four years ago fighting Indians."

"Oh, I am so sorry, honey," Maude said. "Please forgive me. It seems this is my day for opening wounds."

"It's all right, Mrs. Weinberger," said Polly, a slight smile touching her lips. "There is no way you could know."

Dayton's entire being seemed vibrant with life. This beautiful young woman who had captured his heart was *not* married! Relief washed over him like cool water on a hot day, but then his heart was smitten with burning, stabbing guilt. *Chance Dayton! You ought to hang your head in shame. Polly Temple's husband is dead, and you're glad!*

The mixture of relief and guilt swirled through him like a turbulent river. As he fought to bring his inner emotions under control, he heard Maude Weinberger say, "It is so sad that such a young woman should be a widow. You can't be a day over twenty-five."

"I just turned twenty-six, ma'am," Polly said.

Attempting to comfort her, Maude continued, "Well, with your looks and personality, honey, there will be plenty of opportunities to marry again."

As Polly gave the matronly woman a smile, Dayton's heart was drumming against his rib cage.

After three days had passed, the passengers had begun to feel the strain of the trip. For some distance they rode in silence. Polly sat pensively staring into space. She had been talking to the other women over breakfast about her deceased husband, and her loneliness had been renewed.

As the coach rocked and swayed, she peered through a small gap between the window and its leather curtain, watching the snow-covered prairie roll by. After some time, her head turned toward Dayton, revealing to him the sorrow in her large, brown eyes. When she found his sympathetic gaze upon her, tears welled up and deep creases etched themselves on her brow.

Dayton wanted to take Polly in his arms and tell her he loved her, and that if she would let him, he would make her happy for the rest of her life. But he knew he must restrain himself. Such action this early in their acquaintance would only make him appear a fool. After giving her a look of compassion, he pulled his gaze away and sighed. He wished Polly was not getting off at Bismarck. They would be there sometime the next day.

Up in the box, Jenkins spit tobacco and cussed at the

horses. The morning passed with a routine stop at a way station. They had been on the trail again for just over two hours when Hillyer touched the driver's bulky arm and pointed off to the west. About half a mile in that direction, a lone figure was moving along the bank of the Heart River. The alert shotgunner pulled a pair of binoculars from under the seat and focused in on the man. He was lean and lanky, and he was carrying a saddle. Suddenly, the man saw the coach and began to wave wildly with one arm.

"Looks like somebody in trouble, F.E.," Hillyer said. "Horse must've given out. He's carrying a saddle."

Jenkins swung the Concord off course to meet the man, who was desperately trying to wave them down. As they drew near, Hillyer said, "Hey, it's Marshal Banner from Fort Keogh!"

Chapter Six

Marshal Logan Banner saw the passengers peeping out through the leather curtains as the Concord rolled to a halt. Easing his saddle to the ground, he looked up at the round-faced driver and said, "Howdy, I'm Marshal Banner from Fort Keogh."

"We know," grinned F.E. Jenkins. "My partner and I saw you when we were stayin' in Fort Keogh before startin' this run. Never got to meet you face to face. You're on the trail of that dirty killer who murdered your deputy."

"That's right," replied Banner.

"Horse give out?"

"He's dead. Slipped in a gopher hole and broke his leg. I had to shoot him. I'm needing a ride into Bismarck. Do you have room for me?"

"Sure." Jenkins grinned. "Just throw the saddle up top, and I'll introduce you to the folks inside."

But before the stout-bodied driver could climb down, the door of the stagecoach swung open and Chance Dayton jumped out. He pumped the marshal's hand, glad once again to see the man who had saved his life.

Banner explained what had happened to his horse as Dayton helped him load up his saddle.

After Dayton had introduced Logan Banner to the other passengers and the stage was once again on the trail, the marshal explained that he planned to ride with them only to Bismarck, where he would buy a new horse and be hot on Dakota Smith's trail once again. Dayton offered to let Banner ride free all the way to Fargo if he desired, but the marshal said it would depend on how fast the outlaw was moving. If it appeared that he was getting close to the killer, he would have to close in on horseback.

Just before darkness had totally blanketed the prairie, the Concord pulled into a way station. Dayton's heart was heavy. They would be in Bismarck by noon tomorrow . . . and Polly would be gone.

At dinner, someone brought up the subject of Indians. Dayton advised the passengers that there were extra rifles aboard the stage, along with plenty of ammunition. He hoped, however, that there would be no trouble.

Distasteful thoughts picked at Dayton's mind. Black Claw was still killing whites. Would he attack the stagecoach? If an attack was coming, he hoped it would be after Polly was delivered safely to Bismarck. His mind flashed to North Wind. He wondered if the Indian's leg was healing properly.

Batting her lengthy lashes at the marshal, Melody Rogers said, "Mr. Banner, do you have a family?"

Logan Banner, who appreciated a lovely woman, gave her a crooked grin and said, "Well, yes and no, Miss Rogers."

"What does that mean?"

After swallowing a forkful of potatoes, the gray-haired marshal said, "Somewhere there is a wife who never divorced me, and a son whom I have not seen in twenty years."

"Oh, how dreadful!" exclaimed the saloon singer. "Do you mind telling us how it happened?"

Banner sipped at his steaming cup of coffee and said, "Not much to tell. I was working as a farmhand near the area that is now Denver. My wife, Lee Ann, found life a little dull around the farm. She began seeing a shifty-eyed gambler, name of Duane Vivian. I gave him a good beating when I found out. Told him to stay away from my wife."

The marshal had everyone's attention as he took another sip of the hot liquid and continued. "I tried to make things better for Lee Ann, but it didn't work. She was still seeing Vivian on the sly. About three weeks after our son, Lindsey, had turned nine years old, I came in from the fields one day, and she was gone. She had run off with the gambler and taken Lindsey with her. I haven't seen either one of them since."

"How did you happen to become a lawman?" Hillyer asked.

"Well, I left the farm immediately," replied Banner, wrinkles furrowing his brow. "Started searching for Lee Ann and the boy. Searched for over a year, but they were gone, without a trace. Found myself in Montana Territory when I gave up the search, and a small town there called Harper's Bend needed a lawman. I'd handled a gun a little. Had nowhere else to go, so I strapped one on, stuck a badge on my shirt, and have been marshaling ever since."

"I hear tell you're plenty fast with a gun," said Hillyer admiringly.

"I've managed to stay alive," Banner conceded, lifting the coffee cup again.

Hillyer asked the marshal about some of the stories he had heard concerning Fort Keogh's tough marshal. With modesty, Banner confirmed them.

While the stories were being told, the wind came up and began howling around the way station. Banner

ended his account about the time everyone was finished
eating.

Jenkins said, "Well, Wayne, I guess we'd best go out
to the barn and check on the horses."

The stationmaster went outside with the driver and
shotgunner, and when they returned, everyone was
still sitting around the table. A cold gust of wind whistled through the door as they came in, Jenkins swearing
at the weather. When the door slammed shut, he said,
"Whoops! Sorry, ladies. Forgot where I was. I was just
cussin' that d— ah, *dadburned* wind. Colder'n a mother-
in-law's kiss!"

"Smells like snow," Hillyer added.

Polly spoke up, saying, "Oh, I hope it doesn't get
bad. We've just got to get to Bismarck tomorrow. I'm
so anxious to see my father. I haven't seen him since
just after Will was killed, when Daddy came to Fort
Laramie for the burial. He was commandant at Fort
Buford at the time."

"How long has he been at Fort Abraham Lincoln?"
asked Barbara.

"Not more than a week or so," Polly replied. "He
just received orders to transfer from Fort Buford and
become commandant at Fort Abraham Lincoln."

Dayton's head jerked up.

"Daddy wrote me of his new assignment," she added,
"just about the time I learned of the opening of this
new stage route. I sent a letter back, telling him that I
would be coming to Bismarck."

Polly's words hit Dayton like a bolt of lightning. A
cold, prickly sensation danced down his spine. Polly's
father had to have been Colonel Albert Swain . . . and
there was no way she could know he was dead. Suddenly, Dayton felt sick to his stomach. Recent conver-
sations had stirred the grief over her dead husband.
Now she was unknowingly traveling to Fort Abraham
Lincoln to find her father lying in a frozen, somber
grave.

Dayton laid an iron grip on the turmoil that was rising within him. Polly could not be allowed to enter that fort without knowing. Somebody had to tell her . . . and before they reached Bismarck tomorrow.

The raw, biting wind whipped into Black Claw's tipi as Angry Bear entered. The Oglala chief lay on the earthen floor near the fire, wrapped heavily in buffalo hide. He was being tended to by Singing Bird, his wife.

Closing the crude door, Angry Bear knelt down and said, "You were right, Black Claw. The log building is a relay station for the stagecoaches."

Black Claw coughed, feeling pain deep in his chest. "Did you learn when the stagecoaches will be coming through?"

Nodding, the Indian replied, "They have already begun. A stagecoach was at the station this morning. We burned the feet of the station man before we killed him, and he told us. He told us also that the stagecoach runs from Fort Keogh to the railroad at Fargo. There will be many more stagecoaches when the grass is green."

Hatred blazed from Black Claw's dark features. His dark, stony eyes caught the light of the nearby fire. Hoarsely, he spoke a vow. "We will stop the stagecoach like we stopped the railroad! All white eyes will die!"

Dawn came with frost-bitter cold that knifed its way through the cracks around the windows of the way station, driven by the howling wind. Crouching clouds hung ominously in the sky.

Melody Rogers awakened and blinked at the dull gray light that seeped past the heavy shade covering her window. The tiny room was freezing cold.

The sounds of someone tinkering in the kitchen drifted through to her room, the first one in the hallway, closest to the kitchen. She waited a few moments, enjoying the warmth of her bed. The heavy covers were pulled up around her head, exposing only her face.

Counting to three, Melody threw back the blankets and rolled out of bed. Her breath whitened the air as she pulled a wool robe off a clothes tree and slipped her feet into a cold pair of slippers. A chill swept over her as she stepped into the hallway, tying the robe's belt around her slender waist. Then the aroma of hot coffee reached her nostrils.

Following it to the kitchen, she was surprised to see Chance Dayton standing at the table. Immediately, she touched her hair, saying, "Good morning, Chance darling. I was expecting to see Mr. What's-his-name, the stationmaster."

Dayton was turning up the wick of a coal-oil lantern, filling the murky room with yellow light. The wood was crackling and popping in the stove. "He won't be up for a while yet," Dayton said. "Coffee will be ready shortly. Want a cup?"

"Sure do." Melody nodded, rubbing her arms. "I got a little chilled just getting out of bed and fumbling my way into this robe."

Dayton eyed the woman in the light of the lantern. Her fiery red hair lay loosely on her shoulders. Melody was truly an alluring woman, and her curving figure was as graceful as a doe's. "I'm still cold, Chance," she said, gliding toward him.

Melody slipped her arms around his muscular neck. "If you'll hold me," she breathed, "I'll be warm."

Reaching back and grasping her wrists, he said, "I'm still pretty cold myself. You'll warm up faster if you stand over there by the fire."

Bearing down on his neck, she raised her lips to within an inch of his and said softly, "I've missed you, Chance. Kiss me, and say you have missed me, too."

Separating her wrists from behind his neck, Dayton said, "Melody, I have something heavy on my mind right now."

The dance-hall queen studied his face closely, and said, "Darling, you haven't slept, have you?"

"Not a wink," he replied.

She took a step back, brushed a wisp of hair from her eyes, and said, "What is it? You can tell me."

Motioning toward the table, he said, "Sit down, Melody. Maybe you *can* help. I need a woman's point of view on this."

As Melody lowered her graceful form onto a chair, Dayton placed two tin cups on the table. He poured the hot coffee into the cups, replaced the pot on the stove, and sat down across from her. "On my way to Fort Keogh, I met up with a cavalry detachment. They were escorting a Colonel Albert Swain from Fort Buford to Fort Abraham Lincoln, where Swain was to become the new commandant. I camped with them for a night."

As the words registered, Melody remembered the conversation around the table the night before. "Oh, then this Colonel Swain would be Polly's father?"

"That's right."

"Is there some problem with that?"

"Yes, a big one. At dawn we were attacked by a band of Black Claw's warriors. Colonel Swain was killed."

Comprehension registered on Melody's face. "And, of course, Polly doesn't know it."

"Exactly. There is no way she could." With worried eyes, he said, "Melody, I can't let her ride into that fort expecting to see her father."

Melody's jealousy over Dayton's attraction for Polly had soured her attitude toward the beautiful widow. Polly's feelings meant nothing to her, but feigning concern, she gasped, "Oh, the poor dear!"

"My problem," proceeded Dayton, "is how to break it to her. You're a woman, Melody. If you were in Polly's place, would you want to hear it from the man who saw your father killed, or would it come easier to hear it from another woman?"

Whirling thoughts rushed through Melody's head. Dayton was already attracted to Polly, and if he were to tell Polly of her father's death, the news would most certainly throw her into his arms for comfort. Melody was determined that if any woman were to end up in Dayton's arms on this trip, it would be her. Adopting a mask of compassion, she said, "It would be best if she was told by a woman, Chance. It won't be easy, but I will tell her. Poor thing. I'll cushion it as best I can. If you will fill me in on the details, I—"

"Pardon me," interrupted Barbara Stevens, appearing in a gingham robe. "I was awake, and I smelled the coffee. I didn't mean to eavesdrop, but I heard enough to arouse my curiosity. What's the problem?"

Melody's face stretched wire taut. Eyes flinting, she said caustically, "If you heard more than ten words, you *were* eavesdropping, Barbara. What Chance and I are discussing is really none of your business."

"Hold on, Melody," Dayton said, leaning forward. "Maybe a second opinion would be wise. Barbara is her friend."

Running a hand through her long, straight hair, Barbara gave the singer an annoyed look and said, "Is something wrong with Polly?"

Melody sipped sullenly at her coffee while Dayton filled Barbara in on the situation. The brown-haired woman pulled up a chair and sat down, her face full of concern. "Oh, the poor thing!" she exclaimed in a half whisper when the story had been told.

Dayton ran a palm over his face and said, "I was asking Melody what she thought was best. Should I tell her, or would it be best for one of you women to do it? I want it to be handled right."

"You want my opinion?" Barbara queried.

Dayton nodded.

"It ought to come from you," the mail-order bride stated flatly. "I'll tell you why—but if you disagree and think a woman should tell her, then it ought to be me.

You are right, Mr. Dayton. Polly and I have become friends."

Melody fixed her with cold, penetrating eyes. *Why couldn't plain Jane have stayed in bed?*

Ignoring the redhead's insolent stare, Barbara reasoned, "Why should Polly get the horrible news secondhand? You were there and watched her father die, Mr. Dayton. It is far better that it come from you. I see in your eyes warmth, tenderness, and compassion. I have also noticed that you like Polly very much. In my opinion, you are the person to tell her. However, as I said, I will do it if you would rather not."

"No matter who does it, the task is going to be unpleasant," Dayton said. "But I agree, Barbara, that it should be me. All things considered, that would be best."

Melody was miffed at Barbara's intrusion but masked her anger. Smiling slightly, she said, "Chance, you are such a kind and sweet man, always there to help the down and out. But really . . . I'll be glad to break the news to Polly."

"It's all right," Dayton replied, patting her hand. "I'll handle it. As soon as Polly has had breakfast, I'll take her to one of the back rooms and tell her. When you see me leave with her, you inform the driver what's happening. I don't want to pull out until she has a grip on herself and is ready to travel. She'll probably go on to see her cousin in Fargo."

Rising time came for everyone in the way station. While the stationmaster was preparing breakfast, the passengers dressed and groomed themselves.

Melody hurriedly put on her makeup and fixed her hair. She was determined to find a way to give the bad news to Polly. That little blonde was not going to get into Chance Dayton's arms if she could help it. There had to be a way to lure Polly away from Barbara, although the two were rooming together. . . .

Leaving the buttons on the back of her dress unfastened, the shapely redhead moved to her door and peered down the hallway toward Polly and Barbara's room. Just then, their door opened, and Melody pulled her door shut except for a small crack. She watched Barbara enter the hall and say, looking over her shoulder, "See you at the table, Polly. I'm going to get a head start on a cup of coffee." With that, the brown-haired woman closed the door and moved up the hall.

Melody waited until Barbara had passed out of the hallway and turned into the kitchen. Then, her skirts rustling, she smiled to herself, hastened to Polly's door, and tapped lightly. "Polly?" she said softly. "It's Melody. May I come in?"

"Certainly," came the muffled answer.

Quickly, the dance-hall queen moved in and pushed the door shut behind her.

Smiling warmly, the blond woman said, "Good morning, Melody."

Turning her back and lifting her long tresses, Melody said, "Button me up?"

"Sure." Polly nodded, moving toward her.

While the young widow pressed the buttons into place, Melody said, "Polly, a comment you made at the table last night has caused something to surface that you need to know about."

"Oh? What's that?"

"Finish buttoning me, and I'll tell you."

Ten seconds passed. "There," said Polly. "Now, what do I need to know?"

Turning around slowly and adjusting her hair, Melody said, "You'd best sit down."

Eyeing the redhead dubiously, Polly said, "Sit down? Why? What could be so—"

"Believe me," Melody cut in, "you *need* to sit down."

Shrugging her shoulders, the lovely young widow sat

on the edge of the nearest bed. Blinking with curiosity, she said, "Okay. I'm ready."

Standing over her, Melody began by saying, "You mentioned last night that your father had left Fort Buford to become commandant at Fort Abraham Lincoln."

"Yes."

"He would have been at Fort Lincoln only about a week or so?"

"Yes, but—"

"Is your father Colonel Albert Swain?"

"Why, yes," answered Polly, looking surprised. "How did you know? I don't recall telling Daddy's name."

"Chance was with him a few days ago."

"With Daddy? Where? Why didn't he say something last night? Is something wrong?"

"Look, kid," Melody said, pressing false tenderness into her voice. "Chance met the cavalry detachment that was escorting your father to Fort Lincoln on the trail to Fort Keogh. He camped with them for the night."

Standing up, Polly said, "Melody, what is it? *Has something happened to Daddy?*"

The taller woman laid her hands on Polly's shoulders. "Honey, it's like this. Chance wanted me to tell you. The detachment was attacked by Indians. Your father was killed."

Polly's inscrutable eyes stared at Melody's heavily painted face. Something cold moved up her spine, and her heart seemed to freeze within her breast. The redhead's features became a blurred, luminous oval before her. Working her jaw and searching for her voice, she stammered, "D-Daddy is . . . is dead?"

"Yes, honey. Chance was with him when it happened. He saw it."

Polly bit down on her lower lip. A grisly, hollow feeling possessed her, followed by a hot lump rising in her throat. Tears rushed to her eyes as Melody folded her into her arms. "Go ahead, kid," she said. "Let go and cry."

Polly sobbed heavily for several minutes, speaking incoherently to her dead father. When her weeping began to subside, Melody guided her back to the bed. Polly sat down, and the redhead took a washrag from a table and pressed it into her trembling hand. "Here, honey," she said. "I don't have a hanky."

At that moment the door swung open. Barbara came through, saying, "Polly, what's the matter?" Then her eyes took in the scene. Instantly, she knew what had happened. Barbara's lean jaw tightened as anger welled up within her. Struggling to hold her temper in check for Polly's sake, she said, "Melody, you were wrong to do this. It should have come from Mr. Dayton. He told us *he* would do it."

"He wanted me to!" Melody blustered defensively. "I know him well, and he really wanted me to do it, I tell you!"

Suddenly Dayton appeared in the doorway, shaving soap on his face. Before he could speak, Barbara looked at him and said, "Melody told her, Mr. Dayton."

The muscular man wore boots and trousers and was covered from the waist up only by his long underwear. The top three buttons were unfastened, exposing the dark hair on his chest. He lanced the guilty woman with a cold stare. "If I had wanted you to tell her, Melody," he said with a gravel voice, "I would have asked you."

Grief stricken, Polly sprang from the bed and rushed to Dayton. "Oh, Chance," she sobbed, "did Daddy suffer before he died?"

Dayton did not answer, for Polly broke into uncontrollable sobs. Melody looked on with a clouded face as he tenderly took Polly into his arms.

While he held her delicate, trembling form close to him, Dayton wished the embrace could be under different circumstances. He said softly, "I'm sorry, Polly. I didn't mean for it to come to you in this way."

Suddenly, Melody's expression turned icy. She wheeled and walked to the window, her arms folded rigidly over her breast as she stared through the fogged-up glass.

"Chance," Polly sobbed, her face half buried in his broad chest, "I have to know about Daddy. How did he die? Did he suffer . . . or was he killed instantly?" Her voice trailed off into weakening sobs.

"Death was instant," he said reassuringly. "I saw it happen. Believe me, he felt no pain."

Polly pulled her head up. Searching his eyes through her tears, she took a shaky breath and said, "You wouldn't just say that to make me feel better?"

"No," he replied earnestly. "It's the truth. If you want the details later, I'll give them to you. Right now, let's go out to the kitchen and get some coffee in you." Keeping an arm around her shoulder, Dayton cupped her elbow in the other hand and guided her slowly through the door.

As they moved along the hallway toward the kitchen, she said, "I will want the whole story, Chance. To the last detail."

Pushing the door shut behind them, Barbara, her face a mask of fury, wheeled around. Glaring at the back of the singer's head, she spoke with a voice that hissed like water on a hot iron. "Melody Rogers, my upbringing prevents me from calling you what you really are, but I will at least say that you are a selfish, contemptible, despicable, pernicious *witch!*"

Melody turned slowly to face the other woman. "Watch your mouth," she said, exhaling the words through clenched teeth.

Moving closer to her, Barbara continued, "I know why you did that! You didn't want Polly rushing into Chance's arms when the blow came. Well, you got fooled, didn't you?"

Melody's eyes flashed fire. "You shut your stinking mouth, ugly duckling! I always do things my way."

"No matter who it hurts!" Barbara snarled, her face crimson.

"Chance is *my* man!" Melody said heatedly, "and I mean to keep him!"

"You're kidding yourself!" shouted the slender farm girl. "A glass-eyed bat could see that he doesn't care anything about you. Besides that, Mr. Dayton is too good for you. He deserves something better than a cheap, painted-up, hip-swinging saloon singer!"

Melody gasped, fury rioting in her head. Her hand lashed out, slapping Barbara's cheek with a violent blow. Instantaneously, Barbara retaliated. Her hand struck the flashy woman so sharply across the face that the report was like a gunshot.

Momentarily stunned, Melody moved back. She shook her head, grumbled a curse, and lunged for the smaller woman. Her fingers sunk into Barbara's hair, scratching her head, and in return, Barbara wildly seized a fistful of red hair. Instantly, the two women were locked in combat. Hissing and grunting, they hit the bed, flopped down hard on the feather mattress, and then rolled to the floor, kicking, biting, and scratching.

It soon became apparent that though she was smaller, Barbara was stronger. When they came to their feet, Barbara swung Melody by the hair, slamming her savagely into a rack of shelves. The rack rebounded against the wall, jarring a mirror loose that hung nearby. The mirror plummeted to the floor with a crash, followed by the rack, which emptied its contents with a loud clatter.

Melody swung a free hand at Barbara's face and missed. The smaller woman, her hand sunk deep in the fiery red hair, planted a foot behind Melody's ankle and tripped her. Breath whooshed from the redhead's lungs as she struck the floor, totally overcome by Barbara's strength and wrestling skill.

As rapid footsteps thundered down the hall, Barbara

clamped a hammerlock on the saloon singer, rendering her helpless. Melody cried out in pain as the door burst open and Dayton appeared, followed by Logan Banner, Wayne Hillyer, and the stationmaster.

Dayton gasped, "What in the world—?"

Barbara looked up and smiled. Her hair, like Melody's, was a wild mess. Breathing heavily, she said, "Melody tripped and fell, Mr. Dayton. I was just helping her up." With that, she jerked the arm that was twisted behind Melody's back, lifting her upward.

Melody yowled and swore, then sucked air through her teeth, gasping, "She's breaking my arm!"

Barbara released her, saying, "Sorry, Melody. Sometimes I don't know my own strength. Too bad you had to trip and fall like that. You really should be more careful."

Melody gave the smaller woman a poisonous look. Then she stiffly elbowed her way past the men. Her dress was tattered and torn. She disappeared into the hall, and seconds later the door of her room slammed violently.

Dayton gave Barbara an appreciative grin. Shaking his head, he said, "Where did you learn to use a hammerlock like that?"

Barbara threw her long, tangled hair back with a toss of her head, smoothed out her dress, and said, "I was raised with four brothers, Mr. Dayton. It was a matter of survival."

Chapter Seven

The big Concord stagecoach rumbled away from the way station with an icy wind lashing it from the north. Lead-gray snow clouds crawled ominously across the plains, moving southward.

Jenkins hunkered into his heavy mackinaw. From the corner of his tobacco-stained mouth, he shouted above the wind, "We may be in for a good one!"

Nodding in response, Hillyer tightened his hat, saying, "Bet the sun's shining in California!"

Inside the coach, Maude Weinberger held a heavy cloth to her husband's mouth as he coughed violently. The cold air seemed to irritate his lung problem. For several moments, Carl spasmed with deep barks that left his chest aching, and sweat beaded his brow.

Maude's face was constricted with worry. Her husband had been coughing up blood, and she knew that was a bad sign. Tucking the buffalo robe tightly around Carl's slender neck, she bit her lip, fighting back fear . . . the empty, frantic fear that her husband was going to die.

Polly leaned across and patted the elderly woman's

arm. "Mrs. Weinberger," she said tenderly, "there will be a doctor in Bismarck. He will be able to help."

Cecil Knowlton produced a flask and extended it to Maude. "He's welcome to some of this, ma'am."

The woman shook her head. "No thank you, sir," she said, trying to remain kind.

Barbara Stevens sat pensively, her mind on the moment she would meet John Swenson. The scratch on her forehead was lined with iodine, and she pulled a lock of her hair forward in an attempt to conceal the wound.

Melody Rogers sat glumly staring into space. Her heavy makeup failed to disguise the mark on the left cheekbone where Barbara's fist had solidly connected. It was turning a bluish-purple color and was slightly swollen.

No one spoke for some time. Then Polly broke the silence by saying, "Chance, I . . . I must know how . . . Daddy died."

Eyeing her tenderly, the ruggedly handsome man said, "Don't you think it would be best if you waited at least till we get to Bismarck?"

Shaking her head, she said, "No. I'm calm now, and I really must know."

While the others listened intently, Dayton told of how the Indians had seemed to spring out of the ground that cold morning. Without revealing that Colonel Swain had been hit in the forehead, he made it clear that the man had died instantly.

Dayton went on to tell of North Wind and of how he had saved the Indian's life. He explained how North Wind had left while he was sleeping, and then told about loading the frozen bodies onto the horses and delivering them to Fort Abraham Lincoln.

Twice Polly started to cry but fought it off. When he had finished, she said, "There is no reason for me to stay at the fort now. I will just go on to Fargo and see my cousin. If there is room for me on the return trip, I will ride back to Fort Keogh and then catch the next stage to Fort Laramie. I've been living with friends there, ever since Will was killed."

"We'll make room for you," Dayton said, smiling warmly.

"There is one thing. . . ."

"Yes?"

Polly's hand went to her mouth. A frown furrowed her brow. "Well, I . . ." Shaking her head and looking at the floor, she said, "No, it really wouldn't be right."

Lowering his head to look her in the eye, Dayton asked, "What is it, Polly?"

Tears were misting her eyes as she met his gaze. "I would like to visit my father's grave . . . but I know it would detain the coach."

"I doubt if anyone here would complain if we held over for an extra hour or so," Dayton said, his eyes roving the faces of the others. "Besides, we need to give Mr. Weinberger time to see a doctor." Finding there was no objection, he added, "We'll rent a buggy, and I will take you from the stage office out to the fort myself."

Polly smiled. "Thank you, Chance. It means more than I can tell you. I will probably never have another opportunity to see the grave."

"I understand." He smiled in return.

The Concord soon swung into the next way station. While the horses were being exchanged, the passengers took their turns at the small outbuildings and then were served hot coffee in the station house.

As Polly emerged from the outbuilding, she saw Melody waiting for her. Bending her head against the cold wind, Melody said, "Look, kid, I just want to tell you that I'm sorry about your father's death. I . . . I guess I was a little hasty in breaking it to you."

With a polite smile, the blond woman said, "It's all right, Melody. We all are a little impetuous at times."

"One thing for sure, kid," the redhead said. "You've got a real friend in the homely little country girl."

Polly nodded. "I know. I only wish you two could make amends. I think Chance would feel better about the whole thing if you did."

If there was anything Melody wanted, it was to get back into Chance Dayton's good graces. He had not spoken to her since the tussle with Barbara. "I'll make a stab at it," she nodded.

Polly leaned into the wind and returned to the station house, where Dayton had a steaming cup of coffee waiting for her. Moments later, Melody came in, took off her coat, and sat down at the large table where crew and passengers were seated. Directly across from Melody sat Barbara.

Polly's attention was on Maude, who was deeply concerned over Carl's worsening condition.

To Dayton, who was in conversation with Jenkins and Hillyer about the pending snowstorm, Melody directed a pouting look that seemed to beg his forgiveness. Their eyes met, but Dayton seemed to look right through her. Swinging her gaze to the plain-featured woman, she said, "Barbara, I . . . I . . ."

Meeting Melody's gaze with quiet composure, Barbara said, "Yes?"

Clearing her throat, the redhead choked out, "I'm sorry about the fracas. I want to apologize."

Holding her face expressionless, Barbara said evenly, "I will accept your apology, Melody. But only after you apologize to Polly."

"I've already done that," Melody assured her. "Just now. Outside."

The men's conversation dwindled, and their eyes focused on the two women. Polly had picked up the last few words, and speaking to Barbara, she said, "Melody did apologize. Everything is all right."

Dayton's face lit up. "Well, good!" he exclaimed. "I'm glad you ladies have made up."

The redhead slid her chair back, rose, and took a few steps to stand behind Dayton. Drooping her eyelids and pursing her lips, she bent down and said, "Do you forgive me, too? I know I've been a bad girl."

Trying not to laugh, Dayton said, "I think you already got your whipping."

Melody felt her face turn warm, but checked the impulse to lash back in anger. Silently, she returned to her chair.

Jenkins and Hillyer finished their coffee and shouldered into their coats. The burly driver bit off a fresh chew of tobacco and said, "Okay, folks. Time to roll. Next stop is Bismarck."

When the passengers had donned their heavy coats, Logan Banner and Polly escorted the Weinbergers out the door, followed by Barbara and Knowlton. As Dayton was pulling on his gloves, Melody moved close and said, "You're really put out with me, aren't you?"

Dipping his chin to look at her through his eyebrows, the broad-shouldered man said tonelessly, "I was."

"Well, now that I have apologized to Polly and to Barbara," Melody cooed, sliding her hands around his neck, "we can kiss and make up."

Pulling free of her clinging arms, he said, "All is forgiven. Come on, we must get aboard. I want to be inside the coach before F. E. works up his first spit from that fresh mouthful of tobacco!"

It was late morning when the stagecoach rocked and swayed to a halt in front of the Great Plains Overland Stage Company's way station at the west edge of Bismarck. The intense cold was deepening, driven by the relentless wind.

Carl Weinberger was made comfortable next to the huge potbellied stove in the station house. Marshal Logan Banner volunteered to walk to the doctor's office and bring the physician to the ailing old man.

Jim Erikson, the stationmaster, loaned Dayton his horse and buckboard for the trip to Fort Abraham Lincoln. As he and Polly drove away together under the threatening, overcast sky, Melody stood at the window and watched.

Shaking his head at the redheaded woman's expression, Jenkins stroked his chin and said, "Long as we're gonna be a while, Wayne, we might as well take us a stroll to the nearest saloon and have a little something to warm our blood."

Before the shotgunner could comment, Knowlton licked his lips and said, "That sounds like a stupendous idea, Mr. Jenkins. Am I invited?"

The stout-bodied driver grinned. "Long as you can pay for your drinks."

As they moved toward the door, Hillyer said, "You two go ahead. I'll be along in a minute." His eyes trailed to Melody, who still stood forlornly gazing out the window.

Jenkins shot a glance at the redhead and then looked back at his partner. Shrugging his shoulders, he nodded and stepped out into the howling weather. The tool drummer followed, closing the door.

That left the shotgunner virtually alone with Melody. Barbara Stevens was there, but she was occupied with Maude Weinberger, who fretted over her hacking husband.

Stepping up beside Melody, Hillyer said softly, "You really have powerful feelings for Mr. Dayton, don't you?"

The curvaceous woman turned slowly, setting her gaze upon him. "Sometimes," she crooned. "At the moment, I think you're devastatingly irresistible." With the swiftness of a cat, she flung her arms around the startled shotgunner and planted a long, lingering kiss on his lips.

When she released him, Wayne Hillyer was totally nonplussed. He blinked, the sweet taste of the kiss still on his lips, and backed toward the door. Stumbling slightly, he put on his coat, clapped his hat on his head, and pulled open the door. Then he raised the hat to Melody and disappeared. With her hands on her hips, she snickered as the door slammed shut.

Polly sat in silence as the buckboard rumbled and bounced over the frozen ground. Her tiny hat had been replaced by a scarf, which covered her head. It was secured by a large knot under her graceful chin. The biting wind lanced mercilessly at the heavy buffalo robe that covered her body.

Fond memories of her father floated through Polly's mind. Colonel Albert Swain had been good to his daughter. There had always been a close and tender relationship between them . . . and now he was gone. Suddenly, she felt very much alone.

She was thankful for the friends at Fort Laramie who had given her a home since Will's death. They and her cousin Louise—her only living relative—were all that she had left in the world. Certainly she and Barbara Stevens could become fast friends if time would allow, but soon the stage would arrive at Fargo, and the two of them would part forever.

And then there was the man who sat beside her. Chance Dayton was so kind and attentive, treating her as though she were a delicate piece of china. Her slightest wish seemed to be his most firm command. Having known her only for a few days, he certainly had no obligation to show such concern for her.

From the corner of her eye, Polly surveyed Dayton's profile against the iron-gray sky. He was quite handsome. The square cut of his jaw, along with his ruggedly chiseled brow, nose, and cheekbones, almost gave him the appearance of a Greek god. There was an air of strength, self-assurance, and determination about him. He was the kind of man who could do anything he wanted and be successful at it.

Chance Dayton, she thought, *why haven't you ever married? You are everything a woman could want in a man—strong, masculine, resourceful, rugged—but so kind, so gentle. No wonder Melody Rogers is attracted to you. Why, I would be, too, if it weren't for . . . for Will. Oh, how I loved that man! His memory is still warm and fresh, even . . . even after these four years.*

". . . enough?"

Polly suddenly realized that Dayton was talking to her. "What's that?" she asked.

Smiling gently, he repeated above the noise of the wind and the rattling buckboard, "Are you warm enough?"

"My feet are cold, but otherwise I'm fine," she answered, her frosty breath being carried away by the wind.

Dayton felt the friendly warmth of her soft, brown eyes, and once again he struggled to restrain his unruly heart. He was falling more deeply in love with her every minute, and holding her in his arms at the way station had enhanced his yearning for her.

The outline of Fort Abraham Lincoln appeared in the distance. Within moments, they were approaching the west gate of the stockade. The red, white, and blue flag above the wall stood out straight, quivering in the stiff wind. A blue-uniformed man appeared on the wall, rifle in hand, and bending his head into the raw wind, he called out, "Yes, sir?"

"Chance Dayton, here, Corporal! I was here a few days ago. Brought in the bodies of the massacred detachment from Fort Buford. The lady and I would like to see Captain Gordon."

"Oh, yes!" answered the corporal, recognizing Dayton. Turning toward the fort, he commanded, "Open the gate!"

Pulling the buckboard to a halt in front of the commandant's quarters, Dayton hopped out and lowered Polly gently to the ground. She took his arm as they crossed the porch and entered the front office.

A skinny young corporal rose to his feet behind the desk and gave Polly an appreciative look. Speaking to her escort, he said, "Nice to see you again, Mr. Dayton. I assume you want to see the colonel."

"Uh . . . we wanted to see Captain Gordon. Tell him—"

"Well, Captain Gordon is now *Colonel* Gordon, sir," replied the corporal. "He was promoted and assigned as our permanent commandant in place of Colonel Swain."

Polly's face tightened at the mention of her father's name.

"Ah! Will you tell him that Mrs. Polly Temple, Colonel Swain's daughter, is here to see him?"

"One moment, sir," the corporal said as he approached the door of the inner office, rapped twice, and entered.

Looking over at the woman he loved, Dayton said, "Are you all right, Polly?"

She nodded, biting on her lower lip.

When the corporal reappeared, he said, "Colonel Gordon will see you now," and ushered them through the door. He introduced them formally to the colonel and exited, closing the door behind them.

Colonel Edgar Gordon was barely over forty. Rising to his feet, he walked around to the front of his desk. Taking Polly's gloved hand, Gordon clicked his heels neatly, and touched his lips to her fingers. "It is a pleasure to meet you, Mrs. Temple," he said sincerely. "On behalf of the United States Army, as well as myself, may I offer my condolences in the loss of your father? He was a great man, a fine officer, and a real soldier. I may have his job, but no man can fill his boots."

"Thank you, Colonel," Polly said softly, giving him a faint smile.

"Mrs. Temple would like to visit her father's grave, if that is all right," Dayton spoke up.

"Why, of course, Mr. Dayton. So good to see you again, sir," said the colonel. "I'll have one of my men escort you to the burial ground."

"That won't be necessary. I know where it is."

"Oh, of course," Gordon said, nodding. "You stayed for the burial, didn't you? Well, then, if I can be of any assistance, please let me know."

Dayton congratulated the man on his promotion, shook his hand, and guided Polly back into the cold. Within two minutes, the buckboard came to a stop at a small area set apart by a white picket fence within the stockade compound. Simple white crosses stood as silent sentinels over the somber graves.

As Dayton lowered Polly to the ground, she asked, "Isn't it a bit unusual, having the cemetery within the fort walls?"

"I asked the same question," replied Dayton. "They told me that the burial ground was originally outside the wall. Black Claw is so filled with hatred for the white men that he was robbing the graves and mutilating the bodies."

Polly nodded wordlessly, running her eyes over the secluded area.

"It's over here," Dayton said, taking her by the arm.

Weaving among the markers, he led her to a row of relatively fresh mounds. The first one was lettered on the cross bar: *Colonel Albert Swain. Killed in battle. November 1876.*

Polly's hand gripped Dayton's arm. Instantly, he put his other arm around her shoulder. The icy wind plucked at the tears that spilled down her cheeks. "Oh, Daddy," she half whispered with quivering lips, "I love you so. I always will. I'll miss you terribly."

Slowly, she turned toward Dayton, drawing strength from his muscular arm. Weeping silently, she laid her head on his chest.

As he held her, she found herself having mixed feelings. The painful grief over her father was still there, but a strange, warm attraction for this kind and gracious man who was holding her in his arms had surfaced. She felt comfortable in Chance Dayton's arms . . . almost as if she belonged there.

Abruptly, she upbraided herself. *I have no right to have such feelings for this man! I stood at the altar and promised myself to Will. I must always keep that promise . . . and I must ever remain true to his memory.*

Lifting her head to look Dayton in the eye, she said, "We can go now, Chance."

As she spoke, a tiny snowflake struck her face.

There were only a few patrons in Bismarck's Lone Eagle Saloon when Dayton pressed through the door after taking Polly back to the way station. Most of the saloon's customers were gathered at one table, and Dayton saw at a glance that Jenkins, Hillyer, Knowlton, and Banner were among them. Angling in that direction, he knocked the snow from his hat by slapping it against his leg.

Jenkins looked up and said, "Grab a chair, Chance. Sit down here and put a little red-eye in your gut. We'll need to be pullin' out directly." While he poured the amber-colored liquid into a shot glass, he asked, "How's Miss Polly? That visit to her daddy's grave help or hinder?"

"Hard to tell," answered Dayton, shaking wet snow from his coat. "She's attempting to put down some lunch at the moment. Looks like we're going to get a real storm, F.E. We'd best hit the trail plenty quick."

Logan Banner spoke up and said, "This town's only got one doctor, and he's twenty miles out in the wilds delivering a baby. Consequently, Mr. Weinberger is still the same. Or maybe a little worse."

"He and his wife ought to hole up here in Bismarck till he gets better," said Hillyer, still feeling the warmth of Melody's kiss. He had not revealed that incident to his companions.

Cecil Knowlton, who clutched his half-empty bottle as though it were the last one on earth, said, "I tell you, if hish wife would lemme . . . lemme give the ol' man some of thish cure-all, he'd git better!"

Jenkins spit again and said, "Chance, the marshal here is thinkin' about leavin' us behind."

Swinging his gaze to the gray-haired Banner, Dayton said, "Oh?"

The marshal fingered his mustache and nodded. "I just learned that Dakota Smith was here yesterday. If I'm this close on his heels, I'm thinking I ought to get a horse and be after him. There's no question he's heading for Fargo. Only thing that's delaying my departure is the weather. It doesn't look too good."

"You're better off in the stagecoach than on the back of a horse in a snowstorm," commented Dayton. "Snow's falling harder every minute." Pausing to down a gulp of whiskey, he blinked against its fire and asked, "How'd you find out Dakota was here yesterday?"

Banner gave a toss of his head toward the man behind the bar. "Bartender."

"Oh."

"Said the sleazy skunk backed down a local hero with his intimidating manner. Had the man on his knees, licking his boots."

Jenkins swore. "That pompous, yella-haired jaybird's gonna meet his match one of these days. Somebody's gonna blow his guts sixty ways from Sunday."

"You're looking at the man who's gonna do it," Banner said huskily, color coming into his lined face. "Dakota Smith is mine. You can bet your last dollar on it."

At that moment, the door opened. Five trail-dirty riders filed in behind a gust of wind and snow. They were swearing loudly at the weather.

Jenkins rose from his chair and said, "Wayne, we'd best get the stage ready. Oughtta make it to the next way station today if we can."

Hillyer stood up, scooted his chair back, and picked up his coat. The other patrons slipped out quickly, casting a wary eye at the boisterous newcomers.

The five dirty men, smelling like wet dogs, made their way to the bar, demanding instant service from the bartender. Jenkins ran his eyes over the faces of his passengers and said, "See you gentlemen at the station. Think I'm gonna try to persuade the Weinbergers to stay here till the old man can get to feelin' better."

"We'll be along soon as we empty these glasses," Dayton said with a grin.

Hillyer was three steps behind Jenkins when one of the five newcomers caught sight of the short, stubby driver in the mirror behind the bar. The man wheeled around with an insolent sneer on his face, blocking Jenkins's path.

"Howdy, Shorty," said the man, who stood head and shoulders over him. "You think the snow'll hurt the petunias?"

This type of situation was not new to the short but stocky Jenkins. Barroom fights seemed to be his lot, and most of them were started because of his size.

"My name's Chet Moore," said the sneering newcomer. "What's yours?"

Hillyer stepped in, saying, "Mr. Moore, why don't you just turn back to the bar and have yourself a nice quiet drink?"

"I wasn't addressin' you, cowboy," rasped Moore. "I was talkin' to Mr. Five-by-Five here."

Jenkins's face was turning from pink to crimson. The tobacco in his mouth was moving rapidly from side to side. "I'm gonna tell you just *once*, Mr. Moore," he said heatedly. "Remove your stinkin' carcass outta my way."

Moore's partners turned around as Dayton and Banner stood up and slowly moved in. Knowlton took his bottle and headed behind the bar.

"I think I ought to warn you, Moore," Hillyer put in. "My partner here packs a wallop akin to the kick of a Missouri mule."

Chet Moore grinned maliciously, exposing a mouthful of crooked, yellow teeth. "Mule's got to connect to hurt you," he said, shifting to one side and then bracing his feet. "I'm too fast."

Jenkins saw Moore haul back his fist to strike, and he ejected a dark-brown stream of liquid tobacco that hit the man square in the eyes.

Moore was instantly blinded by the dark, stinging fluid, and Jenkins's hammerlike fist caught him flush on the jaw, the impact of the blow flinging the man backward like a rock from a catapult. Moore slammed back against the door, bounced off it, and hit the floor with a thud.

Dayton saw that his four friends were poised and ready to fight. "I wouldn't try it, boys," he told them. "You'll end up like Mr. Moore, there."

The foul-smelling foursome eyed each other. There was surrender in the eyes of three of them, but the fourth, a huge man of over two hundred and fifty pounds, had a brassy look in his dark eyes.

"Don't do it, Luke," one of them spoke up. "Let's pick up Chet, if he's still alive, and get out of here."

The huge, dark-eyed man cast a look at the sprawled figure of Chet Moore on the dusty floor, and grunted, "He's still breathin', Billy."

"It's a wonder, Luke," gasped Billy. "That little guy almost tore his head off!"

Jenkins stood silently, rubbing his fist.

Dayton looked the big man square in the eye and said calmly, "Better take Billy's advice, Luke. Pick up your friend and get out while the getting's good."

"Can't do it," Luke replied flatly, squaring his shoulders.

Dayton saw the punch coming and ducked it. The others quickly moved out of the way. Bracing himself, Dayton brought his right fist back and swung it at Moore, putting every ounce of his two hundred pounds into it. The blow struck Luke's jaw with the sound of a flat rock dropping in mud. The big man's head snapped back. On the rebound, Dayton caught him with a stiff left jab and then followed with a second smashing right to the jaw.

Luke staggered back, tripping over the inert form of Chet Moore. He landed on his rump, rolled over, and rose to his feet. Stepping over Moore, he charged. Dayton's timing was off slightly, and Luke's massive shoulder caught him in the midsection. As they both went down, breath gushed from Dayton's lungs.

Instantly, they were back on their feet. One of the newcomers, feeling a bit bolder, said, "Tear him in half, Luke!"

Jenkins stepped toward him, fist balled tight, and said, "You butt out!"

He did. Quietly.

Luke came at Dayton again, but the ex-cavalry officer managed to dodge the fist and pumped three short, choppy blows to the big man's nose. Luke blinked, shook his head, and moved in. A huge, meaty fist glanced off Dayton's head, and he felt its effect.

Dayton pounded Luke's nose again, but then caught a blow on his own jaw that knocked him off his feet. As he rolled and came to his feet again, he saw Moore crawling out of the battle area. Dayton danced away from the big man long enough to clear the cobwebs from his head. He let Luke come straight at him and then sidestepped and chopped him savagely on the ear. Luke howled, staggered, and whirled around.

The muscular Dayton drove four more punches to the man's face in quick succession. Luke swayed and stumbled slightly, but then came back strong. "I'm gonna beat you to a pulp, little man!" he bawled.

Dayton ducked a whistling fist and popped Luke's thick lips, which split and spurted crimson. The huge man put a hand to his mouth, looked at the blood on his fingertips, and eyes bulging, made an animallike roar and came like a wild bull. Dayton met him with a well-aimed blow to the jaw.

Luke went down but rolled over and came up cursing, wielding a curve-backed wooden chair. His eyes looked slightly clouded.

Logan Banner, who had so far managed to keep himself from interfering in another man's fight, took a half step forward, barking, "Put down the chair, Luke!"

With his gaze still fixed on his huge opponent, Dayton spoke to the marshal between gasps. "It's all right . . . Marshal. He's . . . whipped and he . . . knows it. That's . . . that's why he's resorting to the chair."

Luke came like a freight train, swinging the chair savagely, and Dayton ducked as it cut the air over his head. He ducked it twice more, while backing toward the bar. Again the chair whistled. Dayton leaped back as he ducked again, but this time his back touched the bar, and his shoulder crushed against the cowering form of Cecil Knowlton.

Knowlton took a swallow from his bottle and retreated to the end of the bar. The horrified bartender moved with him. This time the chair came in a violent arc from over Luke's shoulder, but the lithe ex-cavalry officer sidestepped in the nick of time.

Wood splintered everywhere as the chair slammed the bar. The big man whirled around to find his opponent and was met with a blow like a sledgehammer to the temple. He felt his knees go watery. In the split second that he seemed to hang there, Dayton chopped him with a wild blow to the jaw, followed by two more.

Luke's eyes revealed his muddled state, and his legs seemed to be made of rubber. One last punch whipped his head sideways, and he dropped to the floor.

Dayton, sucking in air, stood over the unconscious monster. He felt a hand on his shoulder. It was Logan Banner. "I'm going to buy you a drink, then we'll clear out of here," the marshal said amiably. "If I had the money, I'd buy the whole saloon a round—if you'd promise to let me see you in action again!"

With a chuckle, Dayton downed the shot of whiskey

quickly poured by the bartender and then walked unsteadily to where Luke lay in a bloody heap. From the huge man's pockets he extracted a ten-dollar gold piece. Clapping it on the counter, he said to the wide-eyed bartender, "Big Luke wants to pay for the chair he broke." He moved toward the door, his friends following.

Outside, they were met with a swirling curtain of snow. The wind howled fiercely, and the snow-covered horses at the hitching rail looked like wild white beasts. The blizzard was so intense that they couldn't see the buildings across the street.

As the five men stumbled in the direction of the way station, Jenkins hollered above the storm, "We'll have to wait it out, Chance! We'd be worse than foolish to light outta here in a storm like this."

"You'll get no argument from me," Dayton shouted in return. "We'll hole up at the station."

Chapter Eight

The blizzard played itself out late that night, and on the morning of the next day, Jenkins cracked his whip and headed the four-horse team into the brilliance of the rising sun. The sky was clear, and the air was bitter cold.

Bismarck's physician had not yet returned to town. Jenkins and Dayton tried to persuade the Weinbergers to stay behind, but Carl insisted they go. He was sure he would feel better when they reached Fargo.

Snowdrifts six to eight feet deep had piled up against buildings and alongside fences and gullies, but the powerful wind had swept the plains, leaving the snow there an average of only twelve inches. A cold breeze whipped gusts of dry snow across the prairie's level floor as the Concord cut a path in the broad expanse of white.

The stagecoach made two relay stops that day, and at each the driver and his guard could see that Carl Weinberger was definitely growing weaker. Polly and Barbara did their best to encourage his elderly wife, but Maude was fast losing faith.

The farther the coach traveled, the less snow was on the ground. The wheels of the coach were running in about eight inches of it when Wayne Hillyer glanced at the midafternoon sky and pulled a map from under the seat. He unfolded it and ran the tip of his forefinger along a red line. Then he lifted his eyes and studied the prairie. "We can't be more than a couple of miles from the next stop," he said to Jenkins.

"I hope so," replied Jenkins. "I'm hungry."

At that moment the Concord was passing by a heavily wooded area. Suddenly, from out of the trees, a band of mounted Oglala Sioux warriors came howling across the snow-blanketed ground.

Hillyer seized his shotgun, shouting, *"Indians!"*

Jenkins saw them coming, too, and cracked his whip over the horses' heads. Inside the coach there was immediate excitement as the vehicle picked up speed. Rifles appeared at both windows, shouldered by Dayton and Banner.

The Sioux thundered toward the speeding coach, riding low along the necks of their mounts, rifles ready. Hillyer fired first, and Dayton and Banner followed suit. Indian lead began chewing into the wood of the coach. Inside, everyone was lying low. Knowlton spilled whiskey down his neck attempting to get a mouthful, while Carl Weinberger went into a coughing spasm.

The charging horde was drawing closer. Hillyer's second shot blew a rider from his horse. Again he brought up his double-barreled shotgun and pushed back the hammers.

Dayton put a bullet into a howling Indian's pinto, and the animal did a somersault, its rider tumbling headfirst to the ground, plowing the snow with his face.

Banner dropped two of the Indians as a third pulled up close, raising his weapon. Seeing the warrior, Hillyer lifted his gun and fired. Instantly a red hole appeared between the Indian's eyes. The impact of the shot toppled him off the galloping horse, causing him to hit the ground with arms and legs flailing like a rag doll.

Dayton put a slug through another rider's heart. When

that warrior fell off his horse, the Sioux leader raised his rifle and shouted a command. The other Indians quickly reined in, but not before another warrior went down.

The fifteen Oglala Sioux still on their horses clustered together and looked back at their fallen comrades, their corpses sprawled on blood-splattered snow.

Angry Bear grunted something indistinguishable and then swerved his dark gaze to the fast-moving stagecoach now pulling away. Looking back at his warriors, he said, "We have attacked stagecoaches before in Montana and Wyoming without losing so many braves. It is hard to aim a rifle from a moving vehicle. I do not understand why the white eyes are so successful this time."

North Wind brought his mount in check. The animal was fighting its bit. He looked Angry Bear in the eye and said, "The snow makes a cushion for the stagecoach. It does not bounce as much as usual."

Angry Bear gave him a dark scowl. He harbored a subdued dislike for North Wind. He could never quite pinpoint the reason, but there was something about the younger brave that rubbed him wrong. When Black Claw had sent North Wind along on this mission, Angry Bear had been a bit disgruntled. This was North Wind's first excursion since sustaining the wound in his leg, and Angry Bear would rather not have had him along.

One of the other warriors pointed a finger at the stagecoach, saying that it was headed for a log building in the distance.

Raising his feathered rifle, Angry Bear shouted, "We must catch them as they leave the stagecoach to enter the building! Kill them all! Kill them all!" He gave a death whoop and led his men at a full gallop.

As the Concord drew within three hundred yards of the way station, Jenkins leaned from his seat and hollered to his passengers, "They're comin' up fast! They'll close in as we pull up at the station, so get everybody inside as quickly as possible. I'll swing the coach along the porch on the right side. Wayne and I will cover you!"

A few seconds passed, then Dayton leaned from the window and shouted up at the driver, "The women will help the old folks into the station. Banner and I will stick with you. Cecil's drunk as a skunk—he won't be any good to us."

"Let's all work our way into the station!" Jenkins called back.

"Agreed!" shouted Dayton. "Logs are thicker than the walls of this Concord."

The screaming Indians were within a hundred yards when the swaying coach skidded to a snow-spraying halt. Driver and shotgunner vaulted to the ground, taking cover and raising their weapons. Polly leapt out of the coach and shouted for someone in the station to open the door as she, Barbara, and Melody half carried frail Carl Weinberger onto the porch. Maude followed, her face ashen, and immediately the station door swung open.

"Indians!" Polly gasped to the stationmaster, who seized his rifle and called to the rear of the building for his son. His wife appeared and guided the women and their burden to a nearby couch.

Gunfire sounded outside as the Indians drew near. A signal by Angry Bear divided the charging band into two groups of seven. They broke away in opposite directions, swerving outward in order to come at the station in a circular fashion. Angry Bear remained alone, out of rifle range.

Marshal Logan Banner drew a bead on one Sioux and squeezed the trigger. The Indian spilled off his horse's back as if he had run into a stone wall.

As guns roared and hooves thundered, clouds of blue-white smoke hung in the subzero air. The stationmaster and his son fired from the slitted shutters that covered the windows.

Inside the stagecoach, Cecil Knowlton was totally oblivious to the battle that was going on around him. Lying across the seat, he tipped up the flask and poured its fiery contents down his throat.

Knowlton forgotten, Dayton and the other men continued to fire from behind the Concord as the Indians made two passes. Bullets chewed into the coach's exposed side, sending splinters in every direction. Dayton took a fast look around the corner of the coach and counted three Indians lying dead in the snow. As the Indians pulled out of rifle range to regroup, he shouted, "Okay, men! Now's the time! Get inside the building!"

Quickly, Jenkins, Hillyer, and Banner piled through the door, Dayton on their heels. The stationmaster guided the men to shuttered windows.

As Dayton peered through a thin opening toward the group of Sioux, he spoke from the side of his mouth. "Everybody all right?"

There was a chorus of affirmative answers. But as Dayton saw the Indians begin another charge, Polly spoke up and asked, "Where's Cecil?"

Dayton's head whipped around. "He's not in here?"

"No."

Dayton pulled his gaze back to the narrow slot just as a teetering shadow passed by. Adjusting his eye to the narrow opening, he focused on the tool drummer. Knowlton was swaying on wobbly legs, stumbling in a daze away from the building and toward the warriors, who were now thundering on horseback toward the station in a wild charge. His hat was tilted on his head, and he was shaking the empty flask, cursing it for not producing more whiskey.

Dayton swore and made a beeline for the door. The stationmaster cried, "Don't go out there!"

"Have to!" the ex-cavalry officer retorted. "A passenger's out there. Those savages'll kill him!"

Instantly, Dayton was out the door, rifle in hand, darting for the drunken man. As he rounded the rear of the stagecoach, he saw the lead Indians raising their rifles, and he shouted, "Knowlton! Get back here!"

Knowlton paused, reeling unsteadily, and half turned. Face flushed, eyes red-rimmed and droopy, he tried to make out who had called him. As Dayton dashed toward him, the charging Sioux opened fire, while guns belched smoke and flame from the shuttered windows of the station house.

Dayton saw two Indians fall off their mounts at the same instant Knowlton's knees buckled. The inebriated man dropped, while bullets plowed the snow all around him. When Dayton bellied down to avoid being hit, he saw Cecil move his head.

Dayton crawled toward the drummer as the screaming Sioux circled to make another pass.

Dayton reached the fallen man, who was gasping for breath. Guns roared again from the station. Seeing two Indians galloping in fast, Dayton swung his rifle into position and fired. One of the warriors stiffened, let out a death cry, and fell from his horse. The second skidded to a halt directly above Dayton as he levered another cartridge into the chamber. Expecting to feel a bullet tear into his body, at any moment, the ex-cavalry officer raised the rifle to fire.

The Indian sat straight-backed on his mount, silhouetted sharply against the frozen sky. Guns were booming, and the thunder of hooves shook the snow-covered ground. Dayton checked his finger on the trigger when his smoke-filled eyes cleared—and produced a clear image of North Wind's face.

Each of the two men's gun muzzles were aimed ominously for the kill. Suddenly, everything stood still for an endless heartbeat as the eyes of the two men locked. They heard no gunfire, no whooping, no thunderous noise. It was as if an unseen hand had carved a small fragment of time out of eternity.

North Wind allowed a smile to curve his lips. Dayton swallowed hard, smiling back. In that momentary silence, the Indian spoke one word: *"Brother."*

Time began its ceaseless motion again as North Wind jerked his horse's head around and kicked its sides with his heels. Amid the boom of guns and shrill yelping, he galloped toward his circling comrades, waving them off with his rifle.

Dayton watched the Indians follow North Wind out of rifle range to the place where another Indian sat his horse, observing the action. The ex-cavalry officer sighed with relief and turned his attention to Knowlton. The drunk man lay still on the blood-speckled snow. His pulseless breast told Dayton that he was dead.

Lifting his gaze toward the Indians, Dayton watched them converse for several moments. North Wind seemed to be arguing with the warrior who had kept himself apart from the others. He gestured in the direction of the way station. Then the argument appeared abruptly to end, and they all rode away.

Dayton bent down and hoisted the body of Cecil Knowlton into his arms. He looked again in the direction where he had last seen North Wind, and noted the six bodies of the dead Sioux scattered in a semicircle. He knew the surviving Indians would come back after dark to claim them.

For a moment, Dayton relived the incident when he and North Wind had faced each other. Then he turned and carried the limp corpse to the station.

The stationmaster dashed outside to meet Dayton, who approached with Cecil Knowlton's body. Logan Banner followed, and Polly Temple and Melody Rogers bumped shoulders in the doorway, both eager for a look at Dayton. Their faces paled as Knowlton's limp form came into view.

As Dayton stepped up on the porch, followed by the stationmaster and Banner, Polly said, "Chance, is he—"

"He's dead, Polly," the brown-haired man said grimly.

"Are you all right?" she asked.

Before he could answer, Melody piped up, "Oh, Chance, darling! Are you all right?"

"I'm fine," he answered both of them, swinging the corpse through the door.

Sam Kubik, the stationmaster, told Dayton to take the body to a back storage room. As Dayton moved through the room carrying the drummer's body, followed by the stationmaster, Barbara Stevens and Maude Weinberger gasped at the sight of the corpse. Dayton hurried through to spare them any more unpleasantness. Maude looked as if she was suffering enough, he decided.

Moments after depositing the body in the storage room, Dayton and Kubik reemerged. Introductions were made by Dayton, since no one had had time to exchange names earlier during the panic of the Indian attack. Ronald Kubik, the fifteen-year-old son of the stationmaster, was sent to the well for water, and his mother, Hattie, a matronly woman of forty, welcomed everyone. She expressed concern for Carl Weinberger, who lay deathly still, wheezing slightly as he breathed. But when she offered to help nurse him through the night to relieve Maude, Polly explained that she and the other two younger women had already arranged to sit in shifts at his bedside. With that, Hattie hurried off, to prepare them all a good meal, she said.

Polly turned to the handsome Dayton and said, "What happened out there, Chance? Why did the Indians leave so suddenly?"

The others, equally curious, joined in.

As everyone took a seat, Dayton sat next to Polly, under Melody's watchful eye, and said, "I told all of you about saving an Oglala Sioux warrior's life on the day . . . the day that Polly's father was killed."

"North Wind," Melody spoke up.

Dayton nodded. "Today, when I bent down to pick up Cecil, two Indians rode down on me. I killed one, and levered the rifle for a second shot. When I looked up and saw the other one pointing his rifle at me, I was shocked to see that it was North Wind. He smiled, called me brother, and rode away. The next thing I knew, he was calling off the others."

"Oh, God bless him!" exclaimed Polly.

"The only thing that worries me," said Dayton, "is that North Wind may have a hard time explaining to his leader, Black Claw, why he called off the attack."

"Do you think they will come back?" Barbara queried.

Chance ran his fingers through his thick brown hair. "Wouldn't surprise me a bit. We'd best keep someone on watch all night."

"You really think they'd attack at night?" Sam Kubik asked. "I thought Indians had some kind of superstition about dying at night. Something about their souls wandering aimlessly and never reaching the Happy Hunting Ground."

"Many of them do," said Dayton. "However, from what I hear about Black Claw, he's not very religious."

Logan Banner chuckled. "You might say that. I'll take the first watch, Chance."

Jenkins volunteered for the second watch, and Hillyer offered to be third.

Sam Kubik said, "I'll take the last one."

"No need for that." Dayton smiled. "You need a decent night's sleep so you can be on the lookout tomorrow, after we're gone. You just see to it that breakfast is ready at dawn, and the horses are harnessed and ready to go."

Angry Bear's face had stiffened as he watched North Wind wheel the horse and raise his rifle, calling the other warriors back from the attack. As they had galloped toward him, Angry Bear's eyes had blazed with wrath and he tensed his angular jaws in fury. North Wind had overstepped his bounds in halting the attack.

North Wind had known the Sioux leader was going to be furious. As he rode toward Angry Bear, he realized that he would not only face Angry Bear's wrath but endure Black Claw's fury as well, for he knew his action would be reported to the chief. Whatever the outcome, North Wind would face it.

He had found it increasingly impossible to swallow Black Claw's bloody philosophy of killing every white man just because he was white. To take the lives of particular whites who were stealing from the Oglalas, or attacking them, did not bother him. But to randomly massacre men, women, and children who meant the Indians no harm was more than North Wind could stomach.

Today's incident had caused this feeling to surface with intensity. He had been sent to kill the occupants of the Fargo-bound stagecoach, people who had no intention of hurting or cheating the Sioux—and one of them had been the man who had saved North Wind's life at the risk of his own. He could not allow his fellow braves to kill this white man. Chance Dayton's unselfish deed had built a bond between them—made them brothers—and North Wind would not forget it.

North Wind planned to tell Angry Bear that he had called the warriors back from the attack because the way station was too well fortified and the men inside were excellent marksmen. Six dead Sioux warriors lay on the ground in front of the station to prove his point.

But Angry Bear's bulging eyes had burned North Wind's craggy face as the warriors reined in. His teeth were bared like fangs as he bellowed, "North Wind takes too much upon himself!"

Running his forefinger in a circle, pointing to the braves encircling them, the object of Angry Bear's wrath answered softly, "North Wind is concerned for the lives of his brothers. The white man's building is like a fort, and the men inside are expert with rifles."

The leader pointed a stiff finger at North Wind. "You assume authority that is not yours!"

Swinging his hand around to point at the Sioux warriors who lay dead in the snow, North Wind said firmly, "Six Oglala Sioux will not see sunrise tomorrow. I do not want those who still live to die also. The whites have too much advantage."

Angry Bear had beaten his chest with one of his fists, his voice filled with fury. "I am in command! I will make decisions! The warriors will fight until I say stop!"

North Wind, remaining calm, had pointed again to the corpses of the red men. "Will you command your braves to join their dead brothers?"

Angry Bear had avoided the eyes of the others. "We will go," he had said heavily. "But you will answer to Black Claw for this deed!"

The Oglala Sioux camp had been moved to within five miles of the way station, and in less than an hour, North Wind stood before Black Claw, who was still ailing. Upon hearing Angry Bear's report, the chief went into a rage. Between coughing spells, he demanded that North Wind give an account of his actions.

The young warrior stood straight-backed and gave his irate chief the same answer he had given Angry Bear, hoping he would accept it. But Black Claw ranted and raved at North Wind for asserting authority that was not his to give.

As the angry chief's insane temper grew, his burning words hissed and crackled in North Wind's face like the popping of a bullwhip. When he had sufficiently scathed the young warrior for his unseemly act, he turned to Angry Bear and said, "At the rising of the sun, you will take two dozen warriors, including North Wind. You will attack the stagecoach after it leaves the station. Kill *everyone* on the stagecoach and burn it!"

Angry Bear nodded with a sinister smile.

Black Claw swung a rigid forefinger at North Wind. Speaking through clenched teeth, he growled, "Upon your return, Black Claw wants to hear that you killed whites in the attack. If not, I will pronounce North Wind a *traitor!*"

Hattie Kubik fed passengers and crew a delicious meal as darkness fell. Carl Weinberger's cough seemed to be worsening, and he was unable to take nourishment. Maude stayed by his side while the others ate; then Polly took her place, so the older woman could eat.

Melody looked on with envy as Dayton left the table early to sit and talk with Polly.

As the broad-shouldered man crossed the large room toward her, Polly felt a warm stirring within her heart. *No!* She told herself. *I must not have these feelings toward this man. I must honor Will's memory.*

Dayton stood over the ailing old man for a moment and then took a seat next to Polly. "I know you have been a source of strength to Mrs. Weinberger," he said warmly. "You are quite a lady."

Polly met his warm gaze, felt her face flush, then looked at the floor.

Dayton's arms ached to hold her. The love he felt for the beautiful blond woman was growing every hour he was near her. He desperately wanted to tell her of his feelings, to kiss her soundly. . . .

Raising her eyes, Polly said softly, "Chance, I wish we could get Mr. Weinberger to a doctor."

"There's one in Jamestown," he responded in a low tone. "We'll be there before noon tomorrow."

The look in her eyes told him that she did not think Carl Weinberger would live long enough to make it to Jamestown. Dayton's gaze inadvertantly went to the ailing man's wife, still at the table, and when Maude's eyes met his, he smiled briefly and looked away.

Maude picked aimlessly at her food, observing the young couple. There was no doubt in her mind that Chance Dayton was enamored of Polly. Maude had seen it practically from the beginning of the journey. The lovely young widow was deserving of a handsome, prosperous gentleman like Chance Dayton, she thought. But Polly seemed to keep her guard up around him. . . .

Was it because she was afraid of coming between Dayton and Melody? Maude ruled that out instantly. Anyone could see that any feelings between those two were all on Melody's part. No, something else was eating at young Polly.

Was it the recent death of her father? Certainly Swain and his daughter had been very close . . . but no again. Dayton had made it clear that Polly could cry on his shoulder to relieve her grief over the colonel's death, but Polly was holding back. It was easy to see that she liked the rugged, good-looking Great Plains agent. However, the word *reserve* was written all over her.

Maude finished her meal and returned to where her ailing husband lay on the couch. Standing over the young couple, she said, "I'll take Carl to our room now and bed him down for the night."

Dayton carried the sick man to the room assigned the Weinbergers by the stationmaster. Melody entered the room to sit with Maude for the early part of the night.

Out in the front room, Logan Banner took the first watch. As the other travelers went to their rooms, he left a single lantern burning low and stoked up the potbellied stove. Sitting down by one of the windows, he watched for movement against the moonlit blanket of snow outside.

In the stillness of the night, Banner's thoughts turned to Jim Chapman. What a good lawman he had been turning into, and what a loyal companion he had been— almost like a son.

Banner shook his head. He would not allow himself to think about Lee Ann and . . . the boy. The pain had not been eased much by the passing of the years. Familiar, haunting thoughts began to crowd in. *Lindsey*. Had he lived to become an adult? Where was he? What kind of man had he turned out to be? The boy had been barely nine when she had taken him. . . . Did he know his real name was Banner? Or had he taken the name of that gambler, Duane Vivian? Surely Lee Ann would not stick the boy with a name like Lindsey Vivian.

He shook his head to clear his thoughts. All of that had been long, long ago. His life had changed drastically since then. He again thought of Jim, and the account of his murder came into his mind. The image of him lying dead in the street with his skull half blown away kept returning, unwanted, like a horrible nightmare. He longed to get on with his mission, to find his deputy's killer.

Maude Weinberger sat on the edge of her husband's bed and studied the heavily painted face of the saloon singer, who sat quietly beside the bedstand. The sound of Carl's labored breathing filled the room, while the flickering flame of a low-burning lantern cast dancing shadows over Melody's features.

Maude's curiosity surfaced. "Melody," she asked, "was there ever really anything between you and Chance Dayton?"

Giving the older woman a coy look, she said, "Well, Mrs. Weinberger, we came mighty close. We were crazy about each other. I was in love with Chance, and I believe he felt the same about me, but . . ."

"But what?"

"Well, I . . . I have always been the flirty kind. I like men around me. I'm not hard to look at, and . . . well, I enjoy their attention."

"Guess you're in the right line of work for that," mused Maude.

Melody smiled. "I think I could have married the good-looking lug, but he was wanting a woman that would only have eyes for him. You know . . . the stay-at-home-and-have-babies type."

"Mmm-hmm," crooned the older woman, casting a glance at her sleeping husband.

"Well, that just isn't my style," Melody continued. "I foolishly told him so, and he quit coming around. To tell the truth, Mrs. Weinberger, I've kicked myself ever since. I'd do anything to have him back."

"Anything? You mean like stay at home and have babies?"

"To have Chance"—Melody nodded—"yes. But he won't believe me now. I even told him this once, when we ran into each other after he broke off our relationship. He still feels something for me, I believe, but he just doesn't trust me."

"Looks to me like he's got a fascination for Polly," interjected Maude.

"Oh, that's just Chance," Melody commented. "He's being nice to Polly because of the grief over her father's death. There's no more to it than that."

Maude wanted to tell Melody that she was kidding herself, but the older woman let it go. The two women fell silent, and the labored breathing of the sleeping invalid again filled the room.

At one o'clock, Polly passed Jenkins in the dim hallway. The driver was on his way to relieve Logan Banner, and Polly was going to the Weinbergers' room to take over in Melody's place.

An hour later, Polly reentered the big front room to find Jenkins straining to look through the window.

"See something out there?" the beautiful woman asked as she dipped water from a bucket and poured it into a glass.

"Thought it was a d— uh, a dadgummed redskin, ma'am," he replied. "But it was just a shadow cast by the moon. Mr. Weinberger all right?"

"He's not good at all," Polly answered somberly. "I'm just getting him some water."

Less than half an hour later, the driver heard weeping coming from the Weinbergers' room. Polly materialized from the dark hallway, and with her lovely features full of sorrow, she said, "Mr. Weinberger is gone, F.E. He just all of a sudden quit breathing."

Jenkins's face constricted. "Aw, I'm sorry. Anything I can do?"

"No. I knew you would hear her crying, so I just came to tell you."

At that moment, Dayton appeared, followed by Hillyer, who was coming to replace Jenkins at the window.

Speaking to Polly, Dayton said softly, "Is it Carl?"

"Yes," Polly said, nodding. "He went quietly in his sleep. Just quit breathing."

Hillyer made a sorrowful comment as Dayton followed Polly to the Weinbergers' room. A blanket had been pulled up over the dead man's face. The stagecoach agent placed a firm hand on Maude's shoulder as she sat on the edge of the bed. When she looked up at him, her face was glistening with tears.

"I'm sorry, ma'am," Dayton said sincerely. "At least I'm glad Polly was with you when it happened. I mean her being a widow, and all."

"Yes," said Maude, patting his hand. "Polly is a wonderful girl. She has been more of a strength to me than she knows."

Moving close, Polly leaned over and embraced the older woman, whispering words of comfort. She tried to persuade Maude to get some rest before morning came and they had to board the stagecoach again. But the grieving widow said she could not sleep, and the two kept each other company for the rest of the night.

Dayton was at the window in the front room when dawn painted the eastern horizon a silver gray. There had been no sign of Indians. At breakfast, Maude asked him if Carl could be buried at the station. He conferred with Sam Kubik, and it was agreed that Carl and Knowlton would be buried side by side in the woods beside the station. The men present would dig the graves after breakfast, and then the stage would pull out. Maude would go on to Fargo and claim Carl's inheritance.

Chapter Nine

The sun had just lifted from the horizon to begin its arc across the sky when Angry Bear and twenty-four Oglala Sioux warriors drew near the way station. Expecting the stagecoach to have left already, their plan was to shoot fire arrows onto the station roof and burn it to the ground. When the heat and smoke drove the stationmaster and his family outside, the warriors would kill them. Once they were dead and the station buildings aflame, Angry Bear and his men would go after the stagecoach, set it aflame with fire arrows and kill the occupants. The Indians would ride away in triumph, leaving behind the mutilated bodies and the burning stagecoach.

North Wind rode on with his comrades, worry creeping into every thought. His decision had been made: He could not continue to slaughter innocent people any longer, no matter what the decision cost him.

Little Squirrel came to mind. North Wind now realized that the young brave had apparently reached the same decision the day he had hidden the farm boy. But it was not the knowledge that he might end up over the torture pit like Little Squirrel that worried North Wind.

If that was to happen, he had told himself, then so he it. The commitment was settled in his mind; his loyalty to Black Claw was superseded by the debt he owed Chance Dayton. What worried him was that, somehow, he had to prevent Angry Bear and his warriors from killing the white man who had saved his life . . . and he had no idea how to do it.

When the way station came into view across the glistening prairie, Angry Bear halted his men suddenly, showing his surprise at seeing the stagecoach still parked in front of the station, its horses hitched to the coach. The leader said something was wrong—coaches always hit the trail at sunrise. North Wind tensed as the other Oglala warriors began to discuss among themselves why the coach would still be there, but then one of them pointed off to the wooded area behind the buildings. A group of people were gathered in a circle among the trees.

At that moment someone in the circle saw the Indians, and they instantly headed for the station house. Angry Bear knew he was too far away to head them off. Turning to his men, he said, "We will not wait for the stagecoach to leave. The white eyes are trapped. We will shoot fire arrows onto the roofs of the buildings and into the stagecoach. As the white eyes come outside, we will kill all!"

Swinging his feathered rifle forward, Angry Bear led his men to a spot just out of firing range and pulled up. North Wind listened with dread as the Indian leader commanded half of the warriors to ready the cloth-wrapped arrows, soaked in oil, that each brave had been instructed to bring. As they nocked the arrows, Angry Bear turned to the other warriors. They would go in with rifles blazing, he explained, creating a diversion. This would allow the braves with bows and arrows to get in close enough to lob their fiery missiles onto the roofs and into the stagecoach.

North Wind knew that Angry Bear had made sure

that he was one of the riflemen. He had been given a brand-new Winchester .44 seven-shot repeater that had recently been stolen from the cavalry.

North Wind's mind was working fast as one of the warriors struck flint and lit a torch. One by one, the men with the arrows would touch them to the torch. When the last one was lit, the charge would begin.

Angry Bear set his dark gaze on North Wind and called him to where he sat his horse, some ten yards from the others. North Wind suddenly knew what he had to do.

His heart drummed against his ribs as he rode alongside the Indian leader. He ran his tongue nervously over his lips.

"North Wind!" barked Angry Bear. "You will wait here with me until the whites come out of the burning building. Then you will charge in and kill! Angry Bear wants to see you kill more whites than the other warriors. You are an expert with a rifle. You have many bullets in your gun. If North Wind does not shed much white blood, he is a traitor to Black Claw and to all Oglalas!"

More arrows were being lit. Glancing at the station, North Wind saw the window shutters swing shut. The man who had saved his life was inside that building.

Angry Bear had pronounced Chance Dayton's doom, and North Wind knew he must act. In one smooth motion, he jacked a cartridge into the firing chamber and backed his horse a few steps away.

Angry Bear's face stiffened when he saw the black muzzle of the Winchester pointing at his chest.

North Wind's loud command came like the growl of a wild beast. *"Drop the arrows, or I will kill Angry Bear!"*

Shock registered on the faces of the warriors. Angry Bear, sitting like a statue on his horse's back, was stunned. The look in North Wind's cold, marblelike eyes, and the threat in his voice, left no doubt that he meant what he said.

Burning arrows began dropping to the snow, giving off a hissing sound as they struck the frozen surface.

Angry Bear eyed the traitor, and his deeply lined face turned to stone. Hatred flashed across his dark eyes. Through his teeth, he warned, "North Wind cannot stop twenty-three braves!"

"If they do not drop all weapons, Angry Bear will not live to know what happens!" North Wind snapped. Still holding the rifle, his eyes on the leader, he repeated his command. "Drop the arrows and all other weapons!"

The shutters at the way station slowly opened, and blank faces appeared, watching in amazement as rifles, bows, arrows, and knives struck the snow. When one brave moved too slowly, North Wind barked his name, telling him Angry Bear would die instantly if there were any tricks. Reluctantly, the brave released the knife and let it slide earthward.

When the entire band, including Angry Bear, was totally disarmed, North Wind said, "It is not my desire to do this. But needless slaughter of whites who mean us no harm is shameful. When white eyes attack the Oglalas or steal from us, I will kill them. But undeserved bloodshed is a stain on the honor of Oglalas."

The morning breeze ruffled the feathers in Angry Bear's full headdress. Letting the fury build within him, he glared at the dissident warrior, venom filling his eyes. When he finally spoke, his words came like an arctic wind. "You will die, *traitor*! Black Claw will hunt you down like a rabid dog! You will die a thousand times worse than Little Squirrel!"

North Wind felt tiny needles stab his spine at the mention of Little Squirrel's ignominious death, but he showed the furious chieftain an impassive face. "Before you go," he said, "North Wind will make one brief explanation. In the station house is a man named Chance Dayton. He spared my life when my leg was wounded. Not only did he spare it, but he *saved* it. At the risk of his own life, Chance Dayton spared nothing to save

North Wind. All white men are not bad. Not all white eyes hate Indians. Chance Dayton is a red man in his heart. He is my brother."

Angry Bear's eyes bulged with pent-up fury. "No white eye is a brother to the red man!" he shouted angrily. "North Wind is a rattlesnake *traitor*! He should remove the warrior's feather from his headband!"

In compliance, North Wind reached up and pulled the feather from the headband, letting the breeze lift it from his fingers. The feather sailed a short distance and then dipped lightly to touch the snow. The breeze swirled it across the frozen surface until it lodged and held in an icy crevice.

"Our talk is over," North Wind said with clipped words. "Ride."

The leader nodded to his braves. Slowly they headed out, leaving the weapons lying dark against the snow.

North Wind noticed that the occupants of the station house had gathered outside, Dayton standing in the forefront.

Although the warriors were now some ninety yards away, Angry Bear continued to sit his mount, North Wind's rifle steadily trained on his heart. Then wordlessly, he tapped heels to his horse's sides. As the animal went into motion, he gave North Wind a malevolent look that promised revenge. Then he pulled away from the brave's unwavering gaze and rode off.

North Wind waited until Angry Bear and his warriors had passed from view. Then wheeling his mount toward the way station, he galloped to meet Dayton and the others who stood waiting.

Dayton smiled when the Indian rode up and slid from his horse. As the two men greeted each other, deep affection for the white man was apparent in North Wind's eyes.

"I don't understand it all," Dayton said, "but I saw what you did."

The Indian returned Dayton's smile.

Shaking his head, the white man said, "North Wind, we saw the torch and the arrows. They were going to burn us out, weren't they?"

The Indian nodded solemnly. "Black Claw gave orders that all whites are to die." He raised a hand, placing it on Dayton's muscular shoulder. "Chance Dayton, you are a brother of North Wind. I could not allow Angry Bear and the warriors to kill my brother."

Deeply touched by the Indian's daring deed, Dayton thanked him for saving his life. North Wind proudly commented that it was the right thing to do. Quickly, he explained the repugnance he felt at Black Claw's random slaughter of whites.

"Black Claw will come after me," he concluded. "If he finds me, I will die the slow, painful death of a traitor. But I have done what I know is right."

Dayton squared his angular jaw with determination. "You will not die at Black Claw's hands, my brother," he said in a positive tone. "You will ride the stagecoach with us. We will take you to Fargo and find a place for you to hide."

North Wind protested, saying, "You must move out quickly, Chance Dayton. My people will be back—maybe Black Claw himself. He has been sick, but his anger will be so hot against North Wind that he may forget his sickness and come with fire in his eye. He is determined to stop the stagecoach route, as he did the railroad. He gave orders for us to kill everyone on this stagecoach and burn it."

Dayton turned and walked his friend to the waiting group. He detected a trace of repulsion on Polly's face when she first looked at North Wind. This man had been in the war party that had killed her father. But soon she became cordial, thanking the Indian for what he had just done to save the lives of all gathered here, including her own.

North Wind was welcomed by the others in the group as well, and they joined Dayton in urging the

Indian to ride the stagecoach to Fargo. Since Black Claw was already bent on stopping the coach, North Wind's presence would not increase their danger. But above all, Dayton concluded, North Wind needed a place to hide, and that could be found for him at Fargo.

The dissident Sioux warrior agreed to go along with the stagecoach, but insisted he ride his pinto at least as far as Jamestown. On horseback, he could keep an eye out for Black Claw's braves, he explained.

While last-minute preparations were being made for the trip, North Wind told Dayton and the Kubiks of the weapons that still lay in the snow. Angry Bear and the others would be back, North Wind said, and the stationmaster and his family would be better able to defend themselves if they were well armed. Thanking the Indian for his consideration, Sam Kubik explained that he and his family had decided to take Chance Dayton's advice and go by wagon to Bismarck for a few weeks, until the problems with Black Claw cooled down. But he would be glad to have the weapons for the journey. With that, he sent his son scurrying to where the abandoned guns, knives, and bows lay in the snow.

Within minutes, the big red Concord was rolling eastward, with North Wind riding behind. Inside the coach, the mood was pensive, and Melody expressed fear of being caught out in the open. But Dayton reasoned that it would be no worse than what would have happened under the fire arrows back at the station, and nothing more was said on the subject.

Polly and Barbara, riding backward as they sat on the forward seat, were trying to comfort Maude Weinberger as much as possible. The widow sat between the two younger women, and each held one of the grieving woman's hands.

Dayton and Banner were glad they were able to move from the uncomfortable middle seat—although both regretted the unfortunate fates of Cecil Knowlton and Carl Weinberger. Dayton sat across from Polly, studying her comely features and falling deeper in love. He was hardly aware of Melody, who sat next to him, clinging to his arm. Logan Banner sat on Melody's other side, facing Barbara, and wishing he were not confined in the stage but on the back of a horse on the trail of Jim Chapman's murderer. The fire of vengeance within him kept his blood hot to kill the man who called himself Dakota Smith.

As the stage bounced along, Polly could feel Dayton's eyes on her. Like magnets, they drew her gaze, and when their eyes met, she felt warmth emanating from the handsome man. She would find herself smiling at him and then quickly look away. *What am I doing?* she asked herself. She wanted to shake herself at the next thought. *I not only enjoy his attention, I desire it! Oh, Will, please forgive me!* She swallowed hard and looked out the window.

Moments later, Polly's gaze drifted to Melody Rogers, who had cuddled close to Dayton, her arm linked with his and her head resting on his shoulder. Melody's eyes were closed, as if she were asleep, but the smug look on her face said differently. The sudden tinge of jealousy pricking Polly's heart brought her more internal strife. *Polly Temple!* she thought. *You have no business being jealous of Melody. She has a right to go after Chance Dayton. He doesn't belong to you.* She returned to her study of the landscape, determined not to look at Dayton and Melody unless propriety demanded it.

The Concord pulled into Jamestown in the early afternoon, trailed by North Wind on the black and white pinto. Dayton reported the trouble with the Sioux, and he explained the need for the Kubiks to abandon the way station. The Jamestown stage agent promised to send men and arms to defend the building. Then he joined passengers, crew, and their Indian guest at lunch and returned with them into the brilliant sunshine to continue the journey.

No one noticed the three unsavory men dressed in mackinaws who stood nearby, leaning against the clapboard building.

Jenkins and Hillyer climbed toward the box as Logan Banner held the door of the coach open for the ladies, offering them his hand as they entered. Dayton stood beside the pinto and listened to North Wind argue his case for following on horseback. Dayton agreed to go along with it until the pinto showed signs of giving out.

He was heading toward the coach when the three strangers detached themselves from the nearby building and approached Logan Banner, who was waiting for Dayton before entering the vehicle. Banner knew he had trouble when he saw the face of the middle man in the trio. The man was around thirty, had a mean look in his eyes, and wore his gun low and tied down.

"Hold on, there, Marshal," he said as he drew near. Squinting and tilting his head, he asked, "It *is* Marshal Logan Banner, ain't it? Fort Keogh?"

Banner studied the hawklike face. There was something familiar about it. He knew this man from somewhere. The other two were strangers.

Jenkins eyed the three men warily from up in the box and then leaned over the edge of the seat and spit.

The hawk-faced gunslinger was chewing on a matchstick. Letting it dangle from the corner of his downturned mouth, he said, "Name's Ferris, Marshal. Ford Ferris. Remember?"

Time slid back for Banner to eight years earlier, when he had arrested Ferris for robbing the bank at Fort Keogh. The time spent in prison had aged the man considerably.

"Yeah," the lanky marshal said, nodding. "I remember."

Dayton stepped closer, eyeing the situation cautiously, as Ferris said, "The day you took me, Banner, I almost drew against you. Remember? Then I thought better of it."

"Mmm-hmm," nodded the marshal. He knew what was coming.

The ugly gunslinger rolled the matchstick to the other side of his mouth. A defiant look crept into his eyes. "Reckon I made me a bad mistake that day, Mr. Lawman," he said with a raw edge to his voice. "Cost me seven years behind bars."

"How do you figure that?" Banner asked, knowing what the answer would be.

"Because I could've taken you."

"Don't count on it," the marshal remarked icily.

"I been kickin' myself all this time, Marshal. Every stinkin' day the shadow of them bars crossed my face, I told myself that when I got out, I'd look you up and square things."

Dayton looked at the faces of Ferris's two cohorts. They were hard cases. No doubt they would have to be reckoned with if this talk turned into a gunfight.

"Me and my friends here, we were plannin' on ridin' west, come spring, just to pay you a visit," Ferris continued. "Looks like you saved us a long ride by walkin' out of that stage office . . . almost like it was predestined. Wouldn't you say, Marshal?"

"Tell you what, Ferris," Banner said curtly, "I'm in a real hurry to get this stage on the trail. Now, you and your pals step back out of the way, and I'll forget that you have detained me. We've got to get going."

Ferris's sharp features went rigid. Teeth bared, he snarled, "I'm callin' you, Banner!"

The iron-jawed lawman regarded Ferris with a cold look of contempt. His lips pulled wire thin. "I woke up this morning in a good mood, Ferris," he growled. "You are on the edge of messing it up. Now, like I said, you move your carcass, and I'll forget this whole thing."

Ferris's eyes turned wild, and his words lashed at Banner with the hiss of a whip. "You are a dirty coward!"

Townspeople who sloshed by in the snow stopped to observe the scene. Jenkins and Hillyer looked down from the box, while the four women inside the stage-coach sat frozen with apprehension. North Wind remained on his horse, watching through dark, stoical eyes.

The hair on the back of Logan Banner's neck was bristling. "I'll give you five seconds to retract your statement," he said, his temper rising.

Ferris's face reddened. He backed up three steps and crouched, his hand hovered over the butt of his gun. "You ain't gettin' no retraction, Banner! I'm givin' you ten seconds to draw!"

As Ferris began counting, Dayton spoke in a whisper to Banner, "I'll keep an eye on his playmates."

Banner nodded as Dayton moved in a semicircle to remove himself from the line of fire. The marshal had already adjusted his coat to expose his gun. Calmly, he moved away from the stagecoach, so that the women inside would be clear of any gunfire.

Still counting, Ferris pivoted to stay in line with Banner. When he reached *nine*, his splayed hand snaked downward.

No one heard the word *ten*. Banner's Colt .44 leaped into his hand, belching fire. Instantly, Ferris's cohorts went for their guns, but Dayton's loud *"Hold it!"* drew their attention from Banner. Both men raised their weapons as Dayton's roared. Two more shots rang out, and then both men slumped to the street, dead.

As the smoke drifted away, the bystanders were able to see Ferris lying on the frozen ground near the other two, his sightless eyes staring skyward. The lifeless hand that had gone for the gun clutched it in a death grip. But the gun was still in the holster.

Banner turned and grinned at Dayton. Instantly, he saw that the stage company agent had been hit. Dayton was examining the torn sleeve of his coat, where the bullet had nicked his arm. Blood was seeping through.

"Hey, one of them got you!" exclaimed the marshal.

Banner's excited words brought Polly from the stage-coach, and Melody came right behind her.

"Oh, Chance, you're wounded!" cried the blond woman.

"It's only a scratch," Dayton said calmly, trying to smile. He was pleased with Polly's concern.

"We need to get you to a doctor," she said, scrutinizing the bloody rip in his sleeve.

Melody squeezed in close, almost shoving Polly out of her way. "Let me help, Chance darling," she spoke in a concerned manner.

Polly threw the redhead a frown as a man stepped out of the crowd and said to Dayton, "Doc Murphy is out of town on a call, mister, but I rent him his office. I can let you into it if there's someone who'll take care of that wound."

Melody's face was already white from the sight of Dayton's blood. This type of crisis was out of her realm.

"I can do it," Polly spoke up. "I have bandaged many a wound at Fort Laramie."

While the man led Polly and Dayton toward the doctor's office, townsmen removed the three corpses. Jenkins climbed down from the box, and after ejecting a string of curse words, said, "I've never seen anyone whip out a gun so fast, Marshal! Whooee! That Dakota Smith is already a dead man. He just don't know it!"

It took Polly five minutes to clean Dayton's wound, which indeed proved to be minor. As she carefully wrapped the bandage around his upper arm, she could feel his gaze on her face. He was sitting on the edge of an examining table, a smile on his lips. His overwhelming presence brought life to her senses. Feigning strict attention to the bandage, she avoided his warm brown eyes, moistening her lips nervously as she worked.

The wounded man felt his heart flutter. He had restrained himself to the limit. This moment, with Polly so close and the two of them alone, was too much. As she gave the bandage a final touch, he said softly, "Polly."

The gentle sound of her name brought her head up swiftly. In an instant, Polly looked into those dark eyes and found herself unable to resist as his right hand touched the back of her head and he pressed his lips on her own. A flood of warmth washed over her body, and she raised her arms around his neck . . . and then she checked herself.

Dayton felt her stiffen slightly, just as he released her. His brow furrowed. "I . . . I'm sorry, Polly," he said quietly. "I shouldn't have done that. I shouldn't have taken advantage of you. Please don't be angry."

Polly's heart was hammering hard and fast, and her legs felt oddly unsteady. Touching her fingertips to the table for support, she said, "I'm not angry, Chance. It's just that . . ."

"That what?" he asked, drinking in her loveliness with his eyes.

Working her mouth helplessly, she said, "It's Will, my husband. . . . I—" Quickly she turned, picked up her coat, and started for the door. Pulling it open, she paused to look back. "Chance, I'm not angry. I just can't explain what is going on inside me. I . . . I'll see you outside."

Leaving Dayton in the doctor's office, Polly hastened into the sunlight and headed for the stagecoach. Melody Rogers was in a flirtatious conversation with Wayne Hillyer, and F.E. Jenkins was telling a joke to Logan Banner when Polly drew near. Maude, who sat inside the coach with Barbara, saw the confused look on Polly's face as she climbed in, and knew something had happened in the doctor's office.

Calmly, the elderly woman asked, "Is Chance all right, dear?"

Polly nodded. "Yes, he'll be fine."

When Dayton appeared a minute later, Banner thanked him for helping in the gunfight and, with a sly grin, offered him a job as deputy marshal of Fort Keogh. Dayton grinned back, commenting that he ran into enough trouble without pinning on a badge.

The Concord, followed by North Wind, pulled into the next way station about an hour after dark. They were now just sixty-two miles west of Fargo, and still there had been no sign of Black Claw.

After the evening meal, Polly obtained salve and material for a bandage from the stationmaster's wife. While the others were engaged in conversation, she changed the dressing on Dayton's arm. Maude quietly observed the strain on the face of the young widow.

Later, when the tired travelers were retiring to their rooms, Maude made up her mind it was time to talk to Polly. As luck would have it, the two of them had been assigned a room together, and Maude had the perfect opportunity to bring up the subject of Chance Dayton.

As the two women climbed into the big feather bed, Polly blew out the light, told Maude good night, and rolled over.

After a few seconds, Maude said, "Polly."

"Yes?"

"I want to thank you for the help you've been in my time of grief."

"You're very welcome," replied Polly. "I went through it once. I know the pain you bear."

A brief moment passed.

"Polly," said Maude.

"Yes?"

"You're bearing some pain right now yourself, aren't you?"

Polly paused, then asked, "What do you mean?"

"Chance Dayton."

Another pause.

"I don't understand."

"Honey, it is written all over him. He's in love with you."

Polly did not comment.

Maude's voice cut the silence again. "I've got an idea you feel the same way about him."

Polly remained mute, her heart pounding in her breast.

"But you're fighting it," continued the older woman. "Something's standing between you and that handsome man, and I think I know what it is."

"You do?"

"The ghost of Will Temple."

Polly's silence confirmed Maude's suspicion.

"Will loved you very much, I'm sure," Maude said. "But he's gone on now. You are still here, and you have your life to live. Do you think Will would want you to spend the rest of your life lonely and unhappy?"

"But, Maude—"

"Polly, you're chained to the memory of your dead husband. It isn't right. You've had enough sorrow and loneliness, and you deserve some happiness. Chance is head over heels about you. Now tell me honestly—you're in love with him, too, aren't you?"

All was quiet for a moment. Then Maude heard a tiny sniff, followed by a choked, "Yes."

Maude reached over in the darkness and patted her face. "Only you can break the chain, honey. Do it before you lose that good, kind man."

Polly's voice came so softly now that Maude had to strain to hear. "But what if I break the chain, and one day I lose Chance just like I lost Will?"

Maude was silent for a moment and then softly replied, "I want you to ask yourself one thing. If you could change the past, would you change having married Will, knowing that he would die so young?"

At the same moment, Dayton and North Wind lay in their separate bunks in the darkness. The Indian spoke up and said, "It is best that I go in a different direction tomorrow. Black Claw is sure to appear before you reach Fargo."

"I can't see what difference it makes," Dayton remarked. "If he's bent on attacking the stage, your being with us will not change anything."

"But it will," came the heavy reply. "He will be angry at you for being a friend to me. You are all in greater danger because of me."

"No one has complained of that," said Dayton. "You saved us, and we want to help you. If we can just make it to Fargo, we'll hide you. When Black Claw gives up the search, I'll see that you are taken far away where you will be safe."

North Wind smiled in the darkness. "Chance Dayton. He is a true brother of North Wind."

"I think it would be best if you leave your horse here and ride in the stagecoach," Dayton added. "He's about done in, and it's over sixty miles to Fargo."

The Indian nodded in agreement.

All was quiet for several minutes. Dayton was getting drowsy, when his friend said, "Chance Dayton, you must answer me one question."

"Mmm-hmm."

"The beautiful lady with the sunshine hair—will she be Chance Dayton's squaw?"

"I sure hope so." Dayton sighed. "I sure do hope so."

Chapter Ten

Wayne Hillyer pulled on his boots, eyeing the sun's rays on the window. He and Jenkins had overslept. The stationmaster had finally awakened them, announcing that the passengers were already eating breakfast.

The shotgunner turned his complaining gaze on Jenkins, who stood before a small mirror scraping soap from his face with a straight-edge razor. "I'll never understand you, F.E.," he said stiffly. "We're already late. Why can't you skip shaving for just one day? All the years we've been working together, you've never let your beard grow for even two days."

"Any other complaints, junior?" snapped the stout-bodied driver, looking at his grouchy partner in the mirror.

"Yeah," said Hillyer, standing on his feet. "Why don't you shave before you put your clothes on? Any normal man strips to the waist to shave. But you—you shave with your shirt and bib overalls on."

Jenkins swore under his breath. "Tell you what, crabapple, why don't you climb back in that bed and get up outta the other side? I'll have you in Fargo in time to spark a little with Melody, if that's what you're worried about."

Pulling the door open, Hillyer laughed and said, "You're just jealous, old boy! Now, hurry it up, will you?"

The sun was slanting downward as the Concord left the way station. Inside the coach, North Wind sat on the center seat, looking out the window, scanning the plains for any sign of the Sioux warriors. Hillyer and Jenkins had their eyes peeled up top.

The passengers and crew were feeling tense, knowing Indians were sure to attack before the stagecoach reached Fargo. To relieve the strain, Polly spoke up and addressed the mail-order bride. "Barbara, I'll bet you're getting excited."

The quiet young woman smiled sheepishly. "I guess you could say that. Maybe *nervous* is a better word for it." Her eyes darted from face to face. Attempting to remove the attention of the passengers from herself, she spoke to the Great Plains agent. "Mr. Dayton, John has never mentioned the size of Fargo in his letters. Do you know anything about it?"

Looking from Polly's face to Barbara's, Dayton replied, "The town's population is about twenty-two hundred, but about two hundred farmers are said to come into Fargo to do their business. There are several business establishments—a bank, two hotels, two general stores, a clothing shop, and four saloons. The largest saloon is the Silver Horse, where Melody will be working."

At the mention of her name, the singer smiled at Dayton and squeezed his arm. Polly suddenly felt a sharp twinge of jealousy. She thought of the soft touch of Dayton's lips on her own the day before. Maude's words echoed through her mind. *Only you can break the chain, honey. Do it before you lose that good, kind man.*

Polly's hands turned into fists. Dayton's love was hers for the taking, she knew, but how could she ever love another man and perhaps lose him, like she had lost Will? Her thoughts were interrupted when Dayton said, "And it's Polly's cousin who owns the hardware store."

"Actually my cousin's husband," she added with a smile.

Barbara glanced at North Wind as he studied the prairie, and the fear of a possible attack froze her spine. To keep her mind off the danger, she addressed Dayton again. "Do you know how the town got its name?"

"Well, it used to be called Centralia," Dayton replied.

"Oh, really?"

"Yes. In 1872 they changed the name to Fargo in honor of my old boss, William G. Fargo."

This brought Logan Banner's attention around. He had been thinking of Dakota Smith, hoping that Jamie Lynn Hargrove was attraction enough to hold the outlaw in town until the marshal arrived. To Dayton he said, "You mean Fargo is named after the Fargo in *Wells Fargo?*"

"The same," Dayton said. "Mr. Fargo is on the board of directors of the Northern Pacific Railroad. It was he who engineered the plan to run the railhead to Centralia, and this put the town on the map. So the day the last spike was driven, the citizens held a big ceremony and officially changed Centralia to Fargo in his honor."

"Does Wells Fargo have a stage line into Fargo?" Banner queried.

"That's the irony of it," answered Dayton. "They don't. They've never even considered it."

Banner grinned and shook his head.

The afternoon passed without incident. Just as the lowering sun touched the western horizon, Hillyer's voice bellowed, "There it is! Fargo's in sight, folks!"

Jenkins cracked his whip and swore at the horses,

spurring them into a gallop. He spit a brown stream and shouted, "Hee-yah! Fargo, get ready. Here we come!"

At the same instant the horses lunged into the harness under Jenkins's whip, a large band of Oglala Sioux warriors topped a ridge two miles to the west. Black Claw halted them, anger and frustration marring his dark face. He coughed heavily, cursing the cavalry patrol that had appeared earlier in the day. It had taken three hours to circle the patrol without being seen and then return to the Concord's trail. They had found the coach, but the pinto carrying North Wind no longer trailed it. The stagecoach would be safe once it reached Fargo, since a cavalry unit remained camped at the edge of town.

Angry Bear said, "What will we do now, Black Claw?"

The stone-faced chief glared toward the diminishing vehicle with dark, vitriolic eyes. "There will be other stagecoaches," he grunted. "But there is no other traitor named North Wind. Black Claw will not rest until the traitor is dead."

It was evident that the people of Fargo were eager for the arrival of the Great Plains Overland's first stagecoach. The setting sun revealed giant banners strung across Main Street and welcome signs everywhere. Children, dogs, and adults scurried about the street as the Concord drew near, and a brass band was hurriedly forming.

Inside the coach, there was visible relief now that the threat of an Indian attack was over. North Wind was perplexed, as well as relieved. Why had Black Claw not sent Angry Bear to capture him? Did he not realize North Wind was inside the coach?

The brakes squealed as the stage hauled to a stop. The brass band, now assembled, began to play. Fargo's Great Plains agent, Hoagy Devlin, came out of the office and crossed the boardwalk. Smiling broadly, he opened the Concord's door. "Welcome, Mr. Dayton!" he said excitedly, as the stage company executive stepped out and shook his hand. Devlin also greeted Marshal Banner warmly when the lawman appeared next, but his smile died when the dark-skinned man with high cheekbones and black braided hair emerged.

"It's all right," Dayton spoke up. "This is North Wind. He is my Oglala brother."

Devlin's smile cautiously returned. He shook hands with North Wind and then helped each of the ladies out of the coach.

As Polly alighted, she said, "Mr. Devlin, could you tell me where I might find Greg Stedham's house? He owns the hardware store, but I imagine he has closed for the day. I'm his wife's cousin—"

"Polly Temple," cut in Devlin.

"Why, yes." She smiled. "I wasn't to be here until the next stage comes in, but—"

"I know, ma'am," said the agent. "I have a message for you in the office. The Stedhams are out of town."

"Out of town?" Polly repeated, a quizzical look on her face.

"I'll get the letter from the office in just a moment, ma'am," Devlin said, helping Maude Weinberger from the Concord.

Dayton started to speak to Polly about Devlin's news when he was approached by Horatio Yelland, chairman of Fargo's town council.

A crowd was building rapidly to greet the first stage of the new line as Jenkins and Hillyer began unloading baggage. Barbara Stevens nervously ran her eyes over the milling faces, looking for the one that fit the description John had given of himself. Meanwhile, Logan Banner scrutinized the crowd for tall, blond men.

Devlin explained to the passengers that Mr. Yelland was going to make a short speech and then they could be on their way. He then entered the office to get Polly's letter.

At the same moment, Melody Rogers was approached by a well-dressed man who seemed in a hurry to leave. After greeting him warmly, Melody turned to Dayton, asking if he would come to the Silver Horse and see her before pulling out tomorrow. He assured her that he would, and she walked away on the saloon owner's arm, laughing gaily and swinging her hips.

Devlin returned and handed the blond woman an envelope that bore her name. While Yelland introduced Dayton to the crowd and began his speech, Polly opened the envelope and read the letter.

Polly, dear—

Greg and I have been called unexpectedly to Minneapolis. Greg's mother is critically ill. Have no idea how long we will be gone. You are to stay at the Fargo Manor Hotel. Your room and meals will be charged to us.

Sorry to miss you, but I know you will understand. Please plan to come back and see us. Give my best to your father.

Love,
Louise

When Horatio Yelland had finished his speech, the crowd began to dissipate. Dayton returned to Polly, eyeing the envelope she was placing into her pocket.

"Anything serious?" he asked.

"My cousin and her husband are in Minneapolis," she replied. "His mother is critically ill. Looks like I'll be on the return trip, unless the stage is booked full."

"I'll *make* room for you," he smiled. "But are you sure you're up to traveling again so soon?"

"I can do it," she nodded.

"I'm going to see about getting us a cavalry escort set up in relays," Dayton said advisedly. "The threat of Black Claw attacking is too dangerous. I'll talk to the commanding officer at the camp just outside of town in the morning. It may take a few days to arrange, so you will get a little rest before we start back."

Polly's attention was drawn to a huge blond man coming along the boardwalk, carrying his hat in his hands. Instinctively, she knew it was Barbara's fiancé. She turned to the brown-haired woman, who was in conversation with Jenkins and Hillyer.

The big man stopped and spoke to Dayton. "Pardon me, sir, did you just come in on the stagecoach?"

"Yes, I did," replied Dayton.

Rolling the hat in his huge, meaty hands, he said, "I'm looking for Miss Barbara Stevens."

Polly, tilting her head toward the woman, said, "That's Barbara, right over there, John."

The big Swede was not ugly, but certainly would not be called handsome. He arched his heavy eyebrows. "You know my name, ma'am?"

"Yes. Barbara told us all about you on the trip. I'm Polly Temple, and this is Chance Dayton."

John Swenson shook Dayton's hand and nodded to Polly, then said, "Excuse me, please."

They watched with anticipation as John walked up behind the small, slender woman with the brown hair. Clearing his throat, he said, "Barbara?"

Barbara wheeled at the sound of her name, and her eyes met those of the huge Swede. Working her tongue loose, she said, "John?"

"Barbara, you're beautiful!" he half whispered.

The woman's face crimsoned as John took her into his arms. Polly's eyes glistened with tears, and seeing this, Dayton placed an arm around her shoulder and squeezed her tight. Polly welcomed it . . . and then felt a pang of guilt.

Bidding Polly and Dayton good-bye, Barbara climbed

into John's wagon, while he loaded her luggage, and then they drove away.

The passengers and crew began moving off toward their lodgings. Jenkins and Hillyer were provided a small room at the stage office, and Polly and Maude took a room together in the Fargo Manor Hotel, which was located in the next block down the street, adjoining the large Silver Horse Saloon. Maude planned to look up the lawyer and move into her house the next day. Dayton and Banner also stayed at the hotel and were assigned adjacent rooms several doors down from Polly and Maude. North Wind bunked in the same room with Dayton.

Polly and Maude joined the men for dinner in the hotel dining room. During the meal, Maude observed the longing for Polly in Dayton's eyes.

Logan Banner announced that he was going on a tour of the saloons after dinner. If Dakota Smith was in town, he wanted him. Dayton offered to go with him, but the marshal told him he would handle it alone.

Dayton and North Wind bid Polly and Maude good night and then headed for their room. Maude noted the longing in Dayton's eyes as he gave Polly a warm smile and then walked down the hall.

After she and Polly had left the dining room and returned to their room, the blond woman turned to the older woman and sighed, "Oh, Maude, what am I going to do?"

The widow eased down on the edge of the bed. Patting the spot beside her, she said, "Come here, honey, and sit down." As Polly did so, Maude took a hand and squeezed it. "All right. I want you to tell me exactly what goes through your mind when you are close to Chance."

"I'm not sure I know what you mean."

"I mean . . . do you want to be in his arms?"

Without hesitation, Polly answered, "Yes. Yes, I do. But—"

"It's that *but* that I'm driving at, honey. Tell me exactly what goes through your mind when you check your impulse."

"Will."

"What about Will?"

"I promised to love him forever."

Looking Polly square in the eye, Maude said evenly, "Polly, you can't let the past rule you forever. I know you loved Will, but he's gone, honey. Death has parted you. If you love another man, you've broken no promises. Certainly you will always have fond recollections of Will Temple. You will revere his memory—even love him. But you must let go of Will if you are to find happiness for the rest of *your* life."

Polly touched Maude's wrinkled cheek. "Thank you. I know you're right. It will take a little time, but I'm going to do it. I'll leave the past behind."

Marshal Logan Banner made sure his badge was not exposed as he entered the Silver Horse Saloon, next to the hotel. The place was large and plush. Melody Rogers had done herself well, he thought. Approaching the bar, he addressed the man behind it. "Could you tell me if a Jamie Lynn Hargrove is employed here?"

"No, sir," came the bartender's reply. "Jamie Lynn works at the Yellow Rose. Next block south, across the street. Right on the corner."

Banner thanked the bartender, and as he turned to leave, he spied Jenkins and Hillyer seated at a nearby table. Angling toward them, he said, "You gentlemen save me a seat. I'll be back later."

"Any word on Dakota Smith yet?" Jenkins asked.

"No, but I'm working on it," replied the marshal. With that, he moved to the door and stepped out into the brisk night air.

As the tall lawman moved down the street, his senses quickened. Jim Chapman's killer was in this town. He could feel it in his bones. *Dakota, when I find you, I hope you resist arrest,* he thought. *I don't want the hangman having the pleasure of killing you. I want it all to myself.*

The Yellow Rose Saloon lacked the size and class of the Silver Horse. Banner pushed his way through the door and peered through the haze of tobacco smoke. He ran his gaze around the dimly lit room, examining faces, but no one answered the description of Dakota Smith. Several flashy women were in the place, some seated at tables. One was on a man's lap, laughing loudly, while another stood beside the piano, where a derby-hatted man with garters on his sleeves was playing a soft ballad.

The marshal approached one of the women as she weaved in his general direction among the tables. Touching his hat brim, he said, "Ma'am, I'm looking for a Miss Jamie Lynn Hargrove."

"Oh, sure, honey," she smiled, looking him up and down. Calling over her shoulder, she said, "Jamie!"

The woman standing at the piano looked up.

"This tall one here is lookin' for you."

Jamie Lynn Hargrove swung her way to Banner. Nonchalantly, she gave the tall, gray-haired marshal the once-over and said, "You lookin' for me?"

"Yes," he nodded, touching his hat brim. "I'm, uh . . . Mr. Logan, from Montana. I understand you are a friend of Dakota Smith."

Jamie rolled her eyes and giggled. "Yeah, you might say that."

"Well, he and I have some mutual acquaintances, and they asked me to look him up when I was in town. I was told you would know where I could find him."

Jamie Lynn was not a novice. Something about this tall stranger smelled like the *law.* Shrugging her bare shoulders, she said, "I ain't seen Dakota in a long time, Mr. Logan. He ain't been around."

But neither was Banner a novice—he was certain the

woman was lying. "Well, ma'am," he said, towering over her, "it's mighty important that I see Dakota. I've got a message for him. If he should drift into town anytime soon, tell him Mr. Logan from Montana is looking for him. I'm staying at the Fargo Manor. If I'm not in my room, chances are I'll be at the Silver Horse."

"Got it," Jamie Lynn said before turning back toward the piano.

At the Fargo Manor Hotel, Dayton sat in the room with North Wind as the Indian pondered his future. The Great Plains agent offered to take him south to Fort Sill, Oklahoma. The army needed Indian scouts, and Dayton knew the commandant of the fort. North Wind was appreciative of the offer, but felt that he could not work with the whites. Not all were like his brother, he said. He thought he might go to Texas, where the Comanches might take him in.

Dayton excused himself, telling North Wind he was going down the hall to check on the ladies. Knocking on their door, he said softly, "It's Chance, ladies. Is everything all right?"

The lock rattled, and the door came open. Maude smiled broadly, and said, "Come in, Chance."

"Oh, I won't bother you," he said, peering past the older woman to look at Polly. "Just wanted to make sure you were okay."

"Tell you what," Maude said with a twinkle in her eye, "I need to go to the lobby for a newspaper. Why don't you come in and keep Polly company for a few minutes?"

Maude was out the door and moving down the hall before he could reply. Dayton stepped into the room and saw Polly seated in an overstuffed chair. The nearby lamp cast a soft glow on her lovely features. Her eyes were filled with melancholy as she lifted them. Nervously, she rose from the chair, as if she intended to cross the room, but the broad-shouldered man stopped her by taking hold of her hand. She did not pull it back, but seemed shocked at his touch, and her cheeks reddened. His strong masculine warmth caused her heart to burst into flame.

Pulling her close, Dayton breathed softly, "Polly darling, I . . . I can't hold back my feelings any longer. *I love you*. . . . I've loved you from the very first moment I saw you. If you feel anything for me at all, please tell me. I won't force myself on you, but if there is an inkling of hope that someday you could feel the same about me, I will gladly wait."

While his dark eyes probed her own, Polly struggled to tell him that she loved him, too. But four years of clinging to the ghost of Will Temple prevented her from easily telling him of her love.

"Chance," she said, lips trembling, "I . . . I . . ."

Suddenly, from down the hall, came the sound of a loud crash. Dayton's head whipped around. "North Wind!" he gasped, as the sounds of skirmish thudded repeatedly. "Stay here," he said, dashing through the door.

As he charged down the hallway, Dayton remembered that his gun belt was looped over a bedpost in the room. At the door he could hear thumping noises and heavy breathing. He bolted through the door to find two wild-eyed Oglala Sioux kneeling next to North Wind on the floor, his hands tied behind his back. One of them was just cinching the knot, and when he saw the intruder, he whipped out a knife and stood up.

Dayton's gaze flashed to the gun in the holster on the bedpost. It was too far away. He saw the Indian charge, raising the knife; Dayton hit the floor, rolling, and the Sioux tripped over him and went down.

The second Indian lunged for him as he rolled to his feet. Dayton slammed a fist into his jaw, and the impact of the blow rocketed the Indian across the room. When the stunned man hit the bed, the whole thing collapsed, and he lay in a muddled heap, shaking his head.

North Wind was wrestling with the ropes, attempting to gain his feet, when the Indian with the knife came at Dayton again. The ex-cavalryman sidestepped and seized the arm that held the weapon. Gripping the wrist and the elbow, he raised his knee and brought the arm down on it savagely. Bone cracked, and the Indian howled, dropping the knife.

Taking advantage of the Indian's distress, Dayton bent down, grasped the knife, and plunged it into the Sioux's heart. At the same instant, the other Indian pulled Dayton's gun from its holster on the bedpost and thumbed back the hammer. North Wind saw the threatening muzzle aim for Dayton and threw himself into the line of fire. The gun roared. Breath gushed from North Wind's mouth as the bullet tore into his chest.

Before the hostile Indian could get the hammer back again, Dayton swooped down on him like a giant bird. He drove the knife full length into the Indian's throat and then whirled toward his fallen friend.

North Wind lay on his back, a growing red spot on his buckskin shirt, his eyes glassy.

"You shouldn't have done that, North Wind," he gasped. "You took that bullet for me."

Pink foam gathered at one corner of the Indian's mouth. Managing a weak smile, he breathed one word: "*Brother.*"

Dayton bit down on his lower lip and pressed the lids closed over the eyes that would never again see a Dakota sunrise.

Heavy footsteps thundered in the hallway, and several men entered the room. One of them was Marshal Logan Banner. Another was the hotel desk clerk. Then Polly slipped quietly into the doorway, sided by Maude. The blond woman sagged against the door frame when she saw that Dayton was all right. He was kneeling over North Wind with his back to the door. Dayton stood up, shoulders drooping, and Polly moved to his side. Looking down at her, his eyes filmed with tears, he said, "North Wind jumped in front of the gun. Took the bullet that was meant for me. The last word he said was *brother*."

Speaking with a comforting tone, Polly said, "At least his death was honorable—not the slow, painful death that Black Claw had planned for him."

Chapter Eleven

After Dayton and Banner had taken North Wind's body to the undertaker's parlor, the marshal suggested that a good stiff drink would be in order. Dayton agreed, and strapping on his gun, he walked Polly and Maude back to their room. Then he joined Banner in the lobby. Together, they entered the Silver Horse. A tinkling piano could be heard above the hubbub as they joined Jenkins and Hillyer. Sitting down, Banner told them of North Wind's death.

Pouring himself a glass of whiskey, Dayton asked Banner, "Any leads on Dakota Smith?"

"Talked to his girl friend," Banner replied blandly. "She works at the Yellow Rose Saloon. Said she hasn't seen him in a long time. The girl's lying—I could see it in her eyes. That snake-bellied killer is somewhere in this town. I just know it."

"So what are you going to do?" Dayton queried.

The marshal's face hardened. "Come morning, I'm tearing this burg apart board by board. That filthy worm is bound to be hiding under one of them."

Moments later, the Silver Horse's owner appeared on a small stage in a corner of the large room. The piano stopped its monotonous tinkling and then sounded out a fanfare.

Raising his hands, the well-dressed man said, "Ladies and gentlemen! I've been telling you for weeks about our new songbird from Denver. Well, I am pleased to announce that she has arrived! She is a bit weary from her long journey, but I have prevailed upon her to do one song for us. This is just to whet your appetite for things to come!"

Swinging an arm toward the side of the stage, he said, "Here she is . . . the Silver Horse's new lady of song . . . *Miss Melody Rogers!*"

Applause, whistles, and catcalls filled the saloon as the vivacious redhead strutted onto the stage. When the piano player sounded the first notes of Melody's song, she dropped her eyelids, placed her hands on her hips, and began to sing in a soft, throaty voice.

The lyrics told of how a woman needs her man. Midway through the second verse, Melody left the stage and moved down among the audience. Slowly, she weaved among the tables, making her way toward Dayton's table. She sang the final lines just when she reached it, and Hillyer crimsoned as she ran the tip of a finger under his chin.

"When a woman finds the man . . . her man . . ." Melody closed the song, *"she will never let him go."*

As the audience broke into applause, she dropped into Dayton's lap and kissed the end of his nose.

Suddenly the applause began to trail off in an irregular manner. Eyes turned toward the entrance, and a strange hush fell over the place. Melody eased out of Dayton's lap.

A tall, slender figure stood silhouetted against the door. His hat was tilted down over his angular face, and two guns rode low on his hips, thonged to his thighs. Bushy blond hair pressed out from under his hat.

Logan Banner's whole body tensed. His blood went

172

hot. He was inching his chair back when a female voice said with a tremor of fear, "It's Dakota Smith!"

The killer's words came crisp and cold. "I understand there's a dude named Logan lookin' for me."

Banner rose slowly to full height. As the image of Jim Chapman's shattered skull flashed across his mind, a fire ignited somewhere deep within him and roared to the surface. His breath felt unusually hot on his lips as he said with a steady voice, "If you *are* Dakota Smith, I'm looking for you. My name's Logan."

"Well, you found me!" snapped the rawboned gunfighter. "What do you want?"

Banner's tin star was pinned to his shirt pocket under his vest, and he showed it to the outlaw. With an iron voice, he said, "You are under arrest for the murders of Jim Chapman, Mike Fleming, and Ted Gates in Fort Keogh. I'm the town's marshal. Jim Chapman was my deputy. You're going back with me to stand trial."

Smith reached up and pushed his hat to the back of his head, exposing his face. A mop of blond hair tumbled onto his forehead. "You ain't takin' me, Marshal," he said insolently, "unless you can outdraw me." His hands now hovered over his guns.

The crowd in the saloon pressed back toward the walls. Dayton, Jenkins, and Hillyer moved only a step or two.

Banner's gaze was riveted to the face of the young gunfighter. He squinted to focus on the features clearly, and then he blinked hard. An iciness suddenly coated his stomach, forming into a cold, solid knot. He was looking at himself twenty years ago. His jaw slacked, and he rasped, *"Lindsey?"*

Dakota Smith's eyes widened. Immediately, Chance Dayton saw the resemblance, as did Jenkins and Hillyer. Jenkins swore under his breath.

A cold prickling crawled over the marshal's skin. It took him a moment to find his voice, and when he did, the words came like chilled molasses. "Lindsey . . . Banner. Dakota Smith is Lindsey Banner!"

"How do you know my name?" the rawboned gun-fighter asked cynically.

"Take a good look at me," Banner said. "I didn't leave my full name with Jamie Lynn. Figured you might know the marshal of Fort Keogh is Logan Banner. I'm your pa, son."

Melody Rogers stood sandwiched in the crowd. Her hand flashed to her mouth as she gasped, "Oh, no!"

The blond-headed man looked in amazement at his father. There was no denying the features were much like his own. "Ma always told me I looked just like you," he said, the hint of a smile touching his lips. "You won't be wantin' to arrest me now, will you, *Pa?*"

Banner swallowed hard, and his eyes turned liquid. "I have to, son," he choked. "You've broken the law. I'm oath-bound. I've got to take you in. But I promise you'll get a fair trial."

The killer's eyes turned cold and dark, holding his father steadily. "Then you'll have to draw against me, Pa. I ain't goin' to no trial. You might as well go for your iron."

The whole crowd stood in shock at what was being played out before them. Icy sweat beaded on the law-man's brow. "Don't make me do it, Lindsey," he begged. "I can outdraw you."

Defiance leaped into Lindsey's eyes. "Nobody can outdraw me," he breathed through clenched teeth. His youthful features broke into sardonic lines.

"Please," said the distressed father, "just reach down slowly and lift your guns out of their holsters with the tips of your fingers."

"Nothin' doin'!" Lindsey snapped. His hands flashed downward.

Banner's draw was like the darting tongue of a dia-mondback rattler. His gun was out, cocked, and leveled before Lindsey could clear leather. The blond man's

174

face stiffened and blanched. He froze with his fingers around the gun butts, amazed at the older man's speed.

"Pull the guns out slowly and drop them," Logan said evenly.

Jim Chapman's killer shook his head. Lifting the guns out of their holsters in a smooth manner, he dogged back the hammers, aiming them at his father.

Anguish pinched the marshal's face. "Please, son," he implored, "I can't shoot—"

"I can!" blustered the youth, as his revolvers roared.

Logan Banner was slammed to his back by the impact of the two .45 caliber slugs.

Gun smoke filled the place as Lindsey Banner ejected a fiendish laugh. In fury, Dayton whipped out his gun, but the killer saw the movement and swung one of his .45s on Dayton. Simultaneous shots racketed the place.

Dayton felt hot lead lance his right side as his own bullet ripped into Lindsey Banner's shoulder. The killer staggered and then raised his guns to fire again. Dayton dropped to one knee.

Jenkins darted forward and flung a chair directly at the killer, attempting to spoil his aim, and as the chair connected, throwing Lindsey off balance, the two guns fired wildly. One of the slugs found Jenkins's shoulder, sending him to the floor.

Taking advantage of the distraction, Dayton balanced on one knee, holding his revolver with both hands. Taking careful aim, he squeezed the trigger. The gun boomed, bucking against his palms, and a black hole appeared instantly in Lindsey Banner's forehead. With his blood splattering the wall behind him, he toppled like a chopped tree.

Dayton turned toward the fallen Jenkins and collapsed. Hillyer sprang to Jenkins's side, and Melody hurried to Dayton.

Someone hollered, "Get Doc Riley!"

A man charged out the door, nearly colliding with the hotel clerk, Frank Norton, who had heard the gunplay from the lobby. "Big shootin'!" the man who was leaving announced. "I'm goin' after the doctor!"

Norton stepped up and looked into the saloon. When he saw Dayton on the floor, with Melody Rogers kneeling beside him and ripping up a petticoat, he wheeled and ran back to the hotel.

In their room, Polly Temple and Maude Weinberger were wondering what the gunshots were about when rapid footsteps sounded in the hall, followed by a knock at the door. "Mrs. Temple! Mrs. Temple!" came an excited, muffled voice.

Swinging open the door, Polly saw the wild eyes of the desk clerk.

"Mrs. Temple," Norton gasped, "there's been a shooting at the Silver Horse! Your friend Mr. Dayton has been hit! I thought you would want to know."

Polly's heart leaped to her throat. "Chance? How bad—?"

"I don't know, ma'am, but he's still alive."

Maude hastened to stay on Polly's heels as the blond woman ran for the saloon.

Seconds later, Polly burst through the saloon door, Maude following. Their eyes fell on the two dead men sprawled on the floor and then swung to the bar, where Jenkins sat propped up, blood spreading on his shirt. Hillyer was trying to tear open the shirt to examine the wound, and the stout-bodied stage driver was swearing, telling him to leave it alone.

Then Polly's line of sight found Dayton. He was lying on the floor beside an overturned table, blood visible on his white shirt just above the beltline. Beside him knelt Melody, holding his hand.

Polly hurried to Dayton and dropped down at his other side. Her eyes glistening, she took his free hand and said, "Chance, darling! How bad is it?"

Her concern pleased Dayton, but it was the word *darling* that touched him. He smiled, eyes full of love, and opened his mouth to speak.

It was at that moment that Melody knew her chances with the handsome man were gone. Instantly resigning herself to it, she said to Polly, "The bullet creased his side, but went on through. The doctor will be here any minute. I put a piece of my petticoat inside his shirt to slow down the bleeding." Rising to her feet, she added, "But Chance will be all right. Especially since you called him *darling*."

Polly looked up and said, "I did?"

Squeezing her hand, Chance asked, "Didn't you?"

The tears in Polly's eyes began to spill down her cheeks. To the wounded man, they were more precious than diamonds. "Yes, *darling*, I did!"

As she spoke, the beautiful blond woman bent down and kissed him soundly.

The departure of the stagecoach for Fort Keogh was delayed for two reasons. First, it would take the cavalry a few days to assemble an escort unit. Second, F.E. Jenkins was not fit to travel. It was already settled that Wayne Hillyer would handle the reins on the return trip, but Jenkins insisted that he could ride shotgun. He would be ready and able to go by the time the cavalry unit arrived.

Two days after the Silver Horse shootout, Dayton walked gingerly through the gate of the white picket fence at the Fargo cemetery, with Polly on his arm. Behind them came Maude, a pallid-faced Jenkins, and Hillyer. The little group made its way among the tombstones and halted where three adjacent, rectangular holes stood yawning in the earth's surface. At the foot end of the graves lay three piles of dirt. Beside each one was a coffin.

Two gravediggers stood a small distance away, looking on, the undertaker waiting with them. A lone figure stood at the head of the middle grave, dressed in black, a Bible in his hand.

While the minister read scripture and spoke of life's natural termination at the grave, Dayton thought of Logan Banner's tragedy. For years he had longed to find his son. When fate had finally brought them together, Banner's life was ended by the hand of that very son. Fixing his eyes on the coffins that bore the bodies of father and son, he thought, *At least they are together in death.*

A hot lump lodged in Dayton's throat as his gaze moved to the coffin that held the body of North Wind. *My brother, my friend,* he thought. *Were it not for you, I would be lying in that box. You are a hero, and I bury you with the highest honor. A man has no greater love than to lay down his life for his friend.*

The broad-shouldered man blinked against the tears that scalded his eyes as the minister's final words filtered into his ears.

"Life," said the man holding the Bible, "has a way of balancing things. These three lives have been claimed by death, but somewhere there are parents rejoicing in the lives of their newborn infants."

The minister closed with a brief prayer. Then at the undertaker's command the coffins were lowered into the earth. A handful of dirt was thrown on each coffin, with the minister's words, "Ashes to ashes, and dust to dust," falling dismally on the cold air.

Jenkins, Hillyer, and Maude conspired to let Polly and Dayton walk alone the quarter mile back to town. As they headed for the gate, Maude paused long enough to say, "Polly, I'm so happy for you."

As the old woman joined the two men at the gate, Dayton looked at Polly and smiled. He thrilled at the touch of the woman he loved, who was clinging to his arm as they walked. Because of his sore side, their pace was slow, and periodically he looked down at the sunlight shimmering in the blond hair not covered by Polly's bonnet. Feeling his eyes on her, she looked up each time and smiled.

About halfway to town, Polly squeezed his arm and said, "I just thought of something, darling."

Elated at the sound of the endearing word on her lips, Dayton said, "What's that?"

"The minister's statement about life balancing things out."

"Go on."

"On this journey, you have lost a friend, North Wind. But you have gained a sweetheart—me."

Dayton stopped, winced slightly from the pain in his side, and took Polly into his arms. "You are my sweetheart?" he asked.

"Mmm-hmm." She nodded with a smile. "If you want me to be."

Dayton's senses stirred from Polly's nearness. Her graceful chin tilted as his mouth came down, and the soft touch of her lips caused the blood to race in his veins. The throb of her heart swelled against his chest.

The kiss was a lingering one. When he finally released her, she breathed in deeply, and said, "Well, I still didn't get an answer. Do you want me to be your sweetheart?"

"That *was* your answer, darling," he said, grinning. "But there's something else we need to discuss about this balance."

"What do you mean?" she asked, studying his eyes.

"North Wind was not only my friend, he was a relative."

"A relative?"

"My brother."

"Well . . . yes, I suppose."

"Then for a true balance, I must gain a relative."

Still held tightly in his arms, Polly gazed up at him.

"A *wife* is a relative, isn't she?"

"Oh, Chance," she breathed.

"Polly," he said, looking deep into her eyes, "will you marry me?"

Polly's eyes moistened, and she felt a shiver dance

down her spine as she slid her arms up around his neck. Burying her fingers in the thick mane on the back of his head, she kissed him long and tenderly.

As the kiss ended, Chance peered into her eyes again and said, "Well, I still didn't get my answer. Will you marry me?"

"That *was* your answer, darling," she crooned, and again her lips went to his as if to confirm her reply.

Four days after the Silver Horse shootout, Hillyer was readying the stagecoach for departure. The sun was nearly midway up in the morning sky, which was a clear blue, without a cloud in sight.

Hillyer looked up as Hoagy Devlin approached. After greeting Fargo's Great Plains agent, the shotgunner listened as Devlin gave him the good news that had just hit town. The army had driven Black Claw farther north. He and his warriors would not be a threat to the stagecoach on the return trip to Fort Keogh, so no escort would be necessary.

When Polly approached the Concord, suitcase in hand, Devlin matched her smile and said, "Good mornin', Miss Polly. Is Mr. Dayton still at Doc Riley's?"

"Yes," she nodded. "The doctor wanted to dress both his and F.E.'s wounds with fresh bandages before they left. I really wonder if F.E. ought to be traveling yet, especially up there in the box."

Hillyer laughed. "F.E.'s stubborn as a constipated mule, ma'am. It was all I could do to convince him I should do the driving. An act of Congress couldn't keep him from ridin' shotgun."

"But can he really do it?" queried the blond woman.

"No doubt about it," Hillyer replied with conviction. "If F.E. says he can do it, he can do it. He's a tough old boy!"

Polly let her gaze drift up the street to Dr. John

Riley's office. On impulse, she decided to go there and walk back with Dayton.

Moments later, she entered the front door of the office and moved through the small unoccupied reception area toward a closed door. Tapping on the door, she said, "Hello! It's Polly Temple!"

The muffled voice of the doctor called back, "Are you alone, ma'am?"

Wondering what difference that would make, she answered, "Yes, I'm alone."

"Then come on in."

Polly opened the door to see Jenkins sitting on the examining table, as the doctor worked on the wounded shoulder. Jenkins was shirtless, and Polly's large brown eyes bulged as they focused on the stage driver's partially bare chest. Her mouth fell open.

"Go back and close the door, would you, miss?" asked the doctor.

Totally stunned by what she saw, Polly nodded blankly, backing toward the open door. As the door clicked shut, the doctor saw the wild look on his patient's face.

Arching his bushy eyebrows, Dr. Riley said, "You mean she didn't know?"

"Nobody knows!" hissed Jenkins. "No stage company would hire me if they knew! They don't hire *women*, you know."

While Polly sat down on a chair to compose herself, the stout-bodied driver explained, "As a girl, I was always a tomboy. I was stronger than most boys, and I dressed like them a lot. Wore my hair short, too. Lots of times I was mistaken for a boy and had to fight like one. When I grew up, it sort of hung with me. A few street brawls taught me that I could whip most men, so when stagecoaches came along, I decided I'd like to drive one. Always loved horses and the outdoors."

As the shock slowly wore off, Polly began to chuckle.

"So I applied for a drivin' job with Wells Fargo," continued the stout woman. "I gave my name, Effie

Jenkins. Was it my fault that the man doin' the hirin' thought, when I said my name, I meant the initials F.E.?"

The beautiful blond woman burst into laughter. "You're telling me that nobody knows?"

"Nobody."

"Not even Wayne Hillyer?"

"Not even Wayne." F.E. grinned. "Most of the time on the trail we sleep in the same bed. Can you imagine the heart attack he would have if he ever found out?"

Polly laughed so hard she had to hold her sides.

Doc Riley explained to Polly that he had sent Dayton down the street to buy bandage material and medicine for the trip.

As Effie Jenkins wrapped herself with the broad fabric she used to strap down her full bosom, she said, "Polly, you won't give away my secret, will you? I would lose my job."

Still chuckling, the blond woman said, "No, Effie. Your secret is safe with me. I'll never breathe a word."

Moments later, Polly and the driver stepped out of the doctor's office in time to see Dayton angling across the street toward the stagecoach. Jenkins bit off a chaw of tobacco and said, "Well, honey, looks like Wayne's got 'er about ready to roll."

Several passengers waited for the command to board as Polly and Jenkins joined the group.

Dayton smiled warmly at Polly and then said to the stout-bodied driver, "F.E., are you sure you're up to riding shotgun? I could do it. You'd be more comfortable in the coach."

"Naw, I ain't ridin' inside no stuffy coach," retorted Jenkins. "I'll handle it all right."

Hillyer guffawed. "Don't worry about F.E., Chance. He's tough. He'll handle it!"

"Okay, everybody," Jenkins said in a loud voice, "let's get aboard. Time to be a-pullin out!"

As the passengers began climbing into the stage,

Dayton slipped his arm around Polly's slender waist and pulled her close to his side. She smiled up at him with love in her eyes.

Looking at Jenkins, Dayton said, "By the way, F.E., Polly and I are getting married when we get back to Fort Keogh, and—"

"Hey, that's great!" Jenkins said. "Congratulations!"

"I'd like to ask you a favor," Dayton continued.

"What's that?"

"I'd be honored if you'd be my best man in the wedding. How about it?"

Jenkins chomped hard on the tobacco wad, throwing Polly a furtive look. The future Mrs. Dayton smiled innocently.

The Great Plains driver was deeply touched by Dayton's request, and tears watered the friendly old eyes. Blinking to ward them off, Jenkins turned, spit in the street, and said with a choked voice, "Sure, son. You bet. I'd be right proud to be best man in your weddin'!"

Dayton helped Polly into the coach and climbed in behind her. The big red Concord headed west out of Fargo with Hillyer cracking the whip.

Hillyer noticed his partner wiping away tears. "Yes, sir, F.E.," he quipped, "you sure are a tough old boy!"

Jenkins gave the man beside him a hard look and, thumbing away one more tear, growled, "Shut up and drive."

★ WAGONS WEST ★

A series of unforgettable books that trace the lives of a dauntless band of pioneering men, women, and children as they brave the hazards of an untamed land in their trek across America. This legendary caravan of people forge a new link in the wilderness. They are Americans from the North and the South, alongside immigrants, Blacks, and Indians, who wage fierce daily battles for survival on this uncompromising journey—each to their private destinies as they fulfill their greatest dreams.

☐ 24408	INDEPENDENCE! #1	$3.95
☐ 24651	NEBRASKA! #2	$3.95
☐ 24229	WYOMING! #3	$3.95
☐ 24088	OREGON! #4	$3.95
☐ 24848	TEXAS! #5	$3.95
☐ 24655	CALIFORNIA! #6	$3.95
☐ 24694	COLORADO! #7	$3.95
☐ 26091	NEVADA! #8	$3.95
☐ 25010	WASHINGTON! #9	$3.95
☐ 22925	MONTANA! #10	$3.95
☐ 23572	DAKOTA! #11	$3.95
☐ 23921	UTAH! #12	$3.95
☐ 24256	IDAHO! #13	$3.95
☐ 24584	MISSOURI! #14	$3.95
☐ 24976	MISSISSIPPI! #15	$3.95

Prices and availability subject to change without notice.

Buy them at your local bookstore or use this handy coupon:

FROM THE PRODUCER OF WAGONS WEST
AND THE KENT FAMILY CHRONICLES—
A SWEEPING SAGA OF WAR AND HEROISM
AT THE BIRTH OF A NATION.

THE WHITE INDIAN SERIES

Filled with the glory and adventure of the colonization of America, here is the thrilling saga of the new frontier's boldest hero and his family. Renno, born to white parents but raised by Seneca Indians, becomes a leader in both worlds. THE WHITE INDIAN SERIES chronicles the adventures of Renno, his son Ja-gonh, and his grandson Ghonkaba, from the colonies to Canada, from the South to the turbulent West. Through their struggles to tame a savage continent and their encounters with the powerful men and passionate women in the early battles for America, we witness the events that shaped our future and forged our great heritage.

☐	24650	White Indian #1	$3.95
☐	25020	The Renegade #2	$3.95
☐	24751	War Chief #3	$3.95
☐	24476	The Sachem#4	$3.95
☐	25154	Renno #5	$3.95
☐	25039	Tomahawk #6	$3.95
☐	25589	War Cry #7	$3.95
☐	25202	Ambush #8	$3.95
☐	23986	Seneca #9	$3.95
☐	24492	Cherokee #10	$3.95
☐	24950	Choctaw #11	$3.95

Prices and availability subject to change without notice.